# *DEAD RECKONING*

## D.A. Dickens

PublishAmerica

Baltimore

First printing

ISBN: 1-4137-3667-X
PUBLISHED BY PUBLISHAMERICA, LLLP
www.publishamerica.com
Baltimore

Printed in the United States of America

*To my father, Charles Morgan Dickens. Thanks, Pop.*

# Prologue
# 1794
# Bay of Bengal, India

They came like thieves in the night.

And they came *en masse*.

As an orange blade of sunlight cracked the dawn sky, the prow of the *HMS Glorious* crashed through the brackish chop at twelve knots, plowing a foamy wake with bold impunity. The ship's towering sails billowed full with imperial pretense, spreading a huge white canvass across the glowing firmament; and when the *HMS Industrious* suddenly emerged from the darkness, a powerful naval juggernaut took shape.

Aboard the flagship *Glorious,* as blasts of sea mist whipped the darkened pilot house, Commodore Bernard Lansing III lifted a long cylindrical viewing device. The warship heaved and rolled across the waves as the British naval commander steadied himself before surveying the coast with one eye.

Lansing's gaunt frame was a crooked silhouette against the orange sky, one boot resting on the freeboard capstan and a salty wind rustling the tails of his red tunic. The English lord could hear the painful moan of creaking wood as he lowered his gaze from the sky to the murky shoreline.

Like the patient stalker, he silently studied the Admiralty's coveted target.

Early dawn crept in from the East and the coast remained sleepy, still at a nocturnal rest. In the first moments of dawn the winding beaches of southern India were a thin ribbon of gold, and the dense jungles beyond the breakers remained cloaked in shades of orange and sorrel. As the vessels drew closer, a rolling veil of dew swirled lazily through the expanse of trees before moving gradually out to sea.

It was more than tropical condensation.

*It is ideal camouflage for my sweeping sickle.*

"Left full rudder!" barked the commodore to his first mate.

"Left full rudder! Aye!" came a crisp reply, plangent in the night air.

As the enormous ship began wheeling east, its rudder swinging hard to port, Lansing again surveyed the murky stretch of beach.

*It was timing that had brought victory at Trafalgar,* thought the British commander, now suddenly feeling a tinge of caution.

*But it was timing that had also trapped us at Yorktown.*

An acrid wind, customary to the season, began moving across the heaving waves; and the moon, still visible in the western sky, shined bright like a silver coin, its argent hue shimmering across the rolling swells.

As the British warships dashed toward the coast, the jungle seemed to stretch and yawn. Nocturnal denizens scurried cautiously through the shelter of vines, and exotic birds began to caw and twitter. Then, as if someone had opened a large curtain, the tip of the sun began to crest and the forest came alive with the howls and shrieks of macaques and spider monkeys. Further up the shore, near the delta of the Ganges, a Bengal tiger lumbered awkwardly along the deserted beach, giant paws kicking wide tracks in the wet sand.

With the pallid leer of a hardened soldier, Commodore Lansing looked up into the sky. Soaring gulls swept across the luminous orange firmament, gently riding the hot winds sweeping down from the Tropic of Cancer.

The landscape belonged in a Medici art gallery.

But the commodore was not filled with pangs of aesthetic enchantment.

Although they'd lost their North American colonies, the British were not persuaded to stem their colonial appetite. The English under Cornwallis were reinventing themselves.

Again.

And by daybreak, ten Union Jacks were cracking fiercely in the Bay of Bengal.

"Bring around her starboard broadside!" barked the British commodore. *"Right full rudder!"*

His order echoed across the freeboard, and the tall shadows again shifted, swinging ominously across the waves.

As the British warships moved into position and dropped anchor, bright green semaphore flags were whisked up towering halyards.

They were a prelude to war.

The twin battle wagons were not alone.

Scattered loosely behind the floating fortresses were six British frigates, additional compliments of King George V and his Royal Marines. Many of these same soldiers, now emerging hastily from damp and creaky hulls, had seen the shores of Bunker Hill and Yorktown. And moments before the first canon was fired, boatloads of seasoned infantry were lowered to the waves on wooden longboats and skiffs, their brassy red coats now clearly visible from the shoreline.

As the sailors continued to disgorge bands of infantry, the commodore aboard *Glorious* reached inside his tunic and withdrew a gold pocket watch. After a quick glance he replaced the fat medallion and turned to his first-mate, eyes bloodshot in the new day.

"Pass the order, Ensign. Fire at will."

The ensign turned and shouted the declaration across the deck: *"Commence firing! Commence firing!"*

Another semaphore flag streamed up the halyard of *Industrious*.

And then all hell broke loose.

As if caught in a storm, the massive ships began to rock and sway. Just as the new day began to crest, tiers of canon shot fire and smoke, and rolls of thunder echoed up and down the sleeping shoreline. The cacophony from 200 guns ripped the misty air, tongues of fire licking clouds of moisture; explosive belts reverberated across the harbor and surrounding villages.

As the enormous platforms performed their dance of war, cairns of steel balls and grapeshot were hurled into the sleeping hills of *Borabi*. Resembling a Viking funeral, Indian junkets anchored offshore were set ablaze, the smoking pyres burning bright in the new day.

And just minutes later fires were spreading throughout the thick *Berrera*, rolling wildly into the hills of *Borabi*.

It was a star-spangled opening salvo.

Royal Marines rode the long swells like Orcas on the hunt, rowing methodically toward the smoky shore, each of their skiffs packed tighter than Washington's men crossing the Delaware. One by one they scampered ashore, dragging their skiffs high onto the sand before quickly assembling into tight marching bands. The British had invented the art of D-Day operations; and today they came ashore uncontested.

As Union Jacks battered the salty air, over 4,000 redcoats began marching into the hills of southeast India, long muskets slung across their shoulders. Leather bandoleers, tied across red tunics, held wads of black powder and weighty musket balls; and as the British ascended into the brush, their black boots sank deep in the dense compost lining the hills.

By late morning the redcoats were deep inside the *Borabi* jungle, their colorful colonial uniforms clashing rudely with the untamed, earth-tone environs.

And the humidity had risen along with the sun.

Providing the right flank for General Horton Wellesley's Royal Marines, the 8th Brigade continued their slow trek toward the outskirts of Calcutta, occasionally swinging dull machetes through the madness of stalks and vines. The deep tracts of *Berrera* provided adequate cover, but little else. Horses whinnied as they pulled heavy cannon through the twisted underbrush, bouncing ponderously along the uneven ground. Pack mules brought up the rear, their mangy backs laden with everything from British Scotch to sleeping cots; and soon the flies came out.

But as the forward scouts moved through the heart of *Borabi*, stopping momentarily to gulp from their canteens, the walls of *Berrera* vines came alive.

The lead horse suddenly whinnied and jumped into a frightened pirouette. The gelding's eyes popped wide with fear, and the terrified beast began to buck wildly, dropping rolls of tent canvass from its back. The animal whinnied with panic and galloped wildly into the brush, ropes dangling erratically behind it.

"Stop that animal!" cried a young captain. "What is wrong with that beast?"

Two infantrymen dropped their muskets and took chase, leaping into the brush, still armed with machetes.

"Hold the line!" barked the captain, leaping through a gnarled thicket and joining the chase. Shortly after dashing through the underbrush, he could see his men up ahead, gathered around the fallen animal.

"What is the problem, Westie?" asked the captain, trotting slowly over.

"It has been bitten, me Lord," replied the young soldier, kneeling. "And by the looks, it was a rather wicked bite!"

The captain stepped closer. "Let me see."

The horse's eyes remained as wide as billiard balls, and it was breathing heavily, sharp gusts blowing from its dilated nostrils. The injury was gnarled and messy. It looked as if the horse had stepped into a powerful bear trap. A meandering swath of pink flesh was exposed now, and a jagged tract of teeth-marks left deep tears along its hind leg.

"Perhaps a tiger," surmised another soldier, stepping toward the panicked animal. He leveled his machete. "I will put it down, me Lord."

"Make it clean!" barked the captain, moving back to the formation. "Then let's get moving!"

But another sound suddenly pierced the air, a human scream, guttural and agonizing, warbling through the vines. A musket cracked aloud, and then a second.

The captain turned and began running toward his formation, another warbled scream rising in the air.

"I saw it! Over there!" stammered a soldier. "It dragged Timmons off into the brush!"

"What dragged Timmons off?" asked the captain, stepping closer and leveling his bayonet.

"I don't know, me Lord!" spluttered the man nervously. "A tiger, I think!"

"Find him!" barked the captain.

Several men reluctantly took chase, disappearing in the dense foliage; and just seconds later another voice rose in the hot wind, muffled and distant. "I've got him, me Lord! Over here!"

The captain ran toward the distant wail, jumping frantically through the underbrush, his eyes looking for the orange stripes of a tiger.

Ahead, Private Timmons was sprawled across the moist ground, a sheen of perspiration forming across his face. His breeches had been torn, and a stream of blood was filling his boot. It looked as if someone had taken a machete to him.

"I don't feel very good, sir," muttered the soldier before swooning into unconsciousness.

"Lassiter!" called the captain to a medic. "Get over here quickly!"

The captain's eyes then drifted to the blue cracks of sky through the canopy of vines. "Prepare a stretcher! We need to be twenty miles inland by nightfall! Keep your bloody muskets loaded, and keep a sharp eye! Those bayonets are there for a reason!"

But British 8th Brigade would never meet up with Wellesley's main body of infantry.

The creatures began running through the trees in a disjointed hoard, closing around the redcoats like a pack of hungry hyenas.

But they were not hyenas.

Nor tigers.

And although it would some day be learned that they possessed a four-chamber heart, as well as a 99.3 body temperature, they were not considered warm-blooded mammals at all.

Nor reptiles.

Nor birds.

The ancient Hittites had called them the *helldwado,* an Aramaic term for ground dwellers, and to the ancient Greeks they were known as the escorts across the River Styx. But few through the Age of Imperialism had ever seen anything like them.

And as the crack of muskets rang aloud, the *Berrera* vines shook and swayed. Men were shouting, screaming, and the teeth of their bayonets flickered wildly in the underbrush. But soon the panicked shouts fell silent, and the only sound was the tearing of fabric as their uniforms were partially removed.

Then the bloody squelch of tearing flesh.

As Wellesley's main-body of infantry reached Calcutta and surrounded the city, the mutilated remains of the 8th Brigade were dragged deep into the *Berrera* vines of the *Borabi* forest.

The Admiralty had ordered an inquiry and investigation into the matter, but it was later concluded that the men of the 8th Brigade had simply deserted; and since their cannibalized remains were never discovered, the case was abruptly closed.

And it would take over two hundred years before the truth became known. But it surely would.

# Book I

# Grim Treasures

# 1
# 2010 A.D.
# Varanasi, India.
# 200 Miles Southeast of New Delhi

The surveyor's truck was parked inside a tall fringe of elephant grass, its hood-mounted bubble light blinking aimlessly in the open wilderness. Behind the truck an American engineer continued peering down a geographic scope, his fingers gently adjusting twin focus bars. The light sensitive *spectometer*, situated high on a *Mercury* tri-pod, was used for establishing construction demarcation lines.

After a long moment the surveyor set the digital locking marker and returned to his truck to grab his tool bag.

Matt Miller had already driven several orange stakes into the damp floor of *Borabi*, and wanted to get the grid marked off as quickly as possible. Other than the fact that the chainsaw crews were rolling through here the following morning, it was getting late, he was getting hungry, and Matt reminded himself of the nocturnal denizens that would be scurrying through the underbrush in a matter of minutes.

This wasn't San Francisco or Boston. Bengal tigers, giant boas, and poisonous asps were just a few of the jungle's residents that could prove deadly if provoked, especially if they happened to be hungry.

*And a stampeding bull elephant would starch the hair on anyone's neck,* thought Miller, pausing to survey his immediate surroundings. His eyes combed through the tall banks of *Berrera,* and he thought he heard the distinct snap of a branch.

After another moment of stillness, Miller grabbed two orange stakes and a wooden mallet before walking about twenty meters into the forest.

To those few Hindus living throughout the countryside, this tract of jungle was much more than an abandoned sprawl of wilderness; it was provincially known as the *Forsaken Land.*

This enormous tangled expanse lining the valley of *Borabi* bordered Nepal and had acted as a natural barrier between the two countries for hundreds of years. Located far from the seat of government at Delhi, where the Council Of States *(Rajya Sabba)* and the House of The People *(Lok Sabba)* ignored the cries of its peasants, the land and its inhabitants toppled into sociopolitical obscurity.

The bristling hills and valleys of these unexplored badlands had long been overlooked by the Council of States due to its *"overgrown"* condition. And after conducting multiple studies into the land's development, *Borabi* ultimately became classified as: *"...hostile and arid. Completely unsuitable for agricultural, residential, or industrial development in any capacity."*

But then came India's groundbreaking legislation, a construction bill which swept through both houses of Parliament; it would become known as the Great Eastern Endeavor. And having recently been granted political clemency, *Borabi* suddenly became the recipient of a deluge of government grants and low-interest loans.

And as the American construction teams went to work, Delhi representatives proclaimed a New Era in India's history.

Initially, however, few Hindus were inclined to flock to *Borabi.* The forbidden jungles had become infamous in more ways than one. For thousands of years the twisting walls of *Berrera* were permitted to snake wildly through the underbrush like an ocean of green vipers; and centuries of resulting deadwood, choked off from sunlight and arable soil, eventually cluttered the floor of the forests in dense piles of natural compost, condemning the area as "impassable," while leaving it highly prone to flash fires.

Here, sunlight never touched the moist ground and, other than the brightly-colored *Borabi* berries, the land yielded little more than bramble and bush, vines and branches, stumps and logs, thorns and infection.

And the tract of wilderness running through the *Berrera Canyon,* 90 miles west of Nepal and Mount Everest, a spot chosen for the train's enormous passenger terminal, was even more inhospitable and unreceptive. Not only was the wooded canyon rife with Malaria breeding mosquitoes, gigantic spotted tics, and hoards of biting deer flies, but seasonal cold spells cursed the land here annually, sapping the soil of its nutrients and turning the agricultural alluvium to clay. The spring mud slides, occurring with officious regularity (and comprising high-speed avalanches of red mud and brown water) kept the seeds of anything new and inviting buried in nutrient-depleted mud and rotting foliage. Long since used as a dumping grounds by the outlying communities, virtually everything, stumps, roots, vines, and branches became entangled with abandoned refrigerators, discarded furniture, televisions and motor vehicles; in short, anything left here quickly became entombed in this gnarl of life and death.

It was clear from the onset that the torrid Himalayan basin would never openly welcome human intrusion.

Especially for something as bold and prodigious as an international railroad.

But near *Alcuoco,* along the meandering valley of Mount Everest, orange *Caterpillar* tractors signaled the coming winds of that magnanimous change.

The big American diesels grumbled and plowed through the tall *Berrera* vines like a herd of steel rhinoceros. With mechanical roars, they continued ripping loose a network of roots and vines from the roving expanse of entanglement, methodically clearing brush, deadwood, stumps and felled trees. At fifteen tons each, the diesel shovels cut a swath through the agricultural nightmare like Sherman Tanks through a strawberry patch; and the dozers worked fast. They had to. These *Caterpillars* represented the vanguard of an operation that was expected to cost more than 100 billion American dollars.

And this level of deforestation involved more than just bull dozers.

Twenty miles south of the *Caterpillars,* and weaving precariously along the narrow dirt roads, were convoys of logging rigs. The flat-bed tractor-trailers, loaded high with timber and stumps, belonged to the Montana logging firm Eros And Sons; and their American drivers, of Teamsters 409, worked around the clock, rumbling in and out of the jungle through dusk and dawn. Sometimes their high-beam headlights, casting eerie flashes of luminescence through the wooded countryside, would trigger a stamped of elephants, or have some other mass migration effect.

This recently deforested madness was planned to become a passenger terminal by 2012.

And just 50 miles further south the concrete embrasures for the southern link were already being poured, and ribbon track was being installed just as soon as the concrete had time to cure.

The entire project, referred to as the Orient Express II by the Americans, had become a multi-national corporate blitz, directed and coordinated by an American railroad company.

But Mark Black, a heavy equipment operator from Pendleton & Waxler Contracting, wasn't worried about deadlines, overtime, or concrete trucks closing fast on his tail. He continued plowing near the Mondava Valley at his usual and deliberate pace, furrowing his oversized behemoth through the overgrown wasteland which lay on the southern fringe of the immense glacier. As Mark pushed aside a felled cedar with his mechanical "bucket," his dozer's tracks firmly straddled the piedmont of the world's tallest mountain.

Heavy equipment was Mark's specialty, and this tour of civilian duty had initially promised perks and rewards well beyond the restrictive reach of OSHA and other labor commissions. The salary was up to scale, and housing and many other provisions were readily provided, making the trip a low-expense opportunity to sock away a few thousand dollars, maybe more. If he played his cards right then he'd be going home with a pocketful of seed money, available capital to launch his baby, a 23' Sea King *The Other Side,* into a challenging trek to the tip of Argentina. It was a trip he'd been planning for the past ten years, a trip his sponsor continually encouraged him to make. And, as far as Mark was concerned, ten years was long enough. It was time to make it. He had arrived.

But Black had not played his cards right, quite literally, and he steadily maintained a smoldering sense of regret and humiliation as the days dragged on.

A sense of failure.

Ever since that drunken night, other than a dozen inoculation shots, a million mosquito bites, and an everlasting case of dysentery or typhus, nothing came with ease here, despite the ridiculous overtime available. The simple truth was that it was no longer a profitable endeavor; at least not for Mark. Besides, he was beginning to miss his home now, his tiny Towson, Maryland apartment, not to mention his favorite recliner, his satellite TV remote-control, and his George Foreman grill.

*I won't be eating out for a while,* Mark quickly reminded himself.

*Good Ole George is gonna get one hella-va work-out!*

That's because Mark Black was broke, totally busted, and it had happened almost overnight. After finding a hot poker game at a supply tent, and feeling that distant charge of compulsion returning, something he'd been able to contain for the past ten years, Black eventually incurred over $12,000 in losses, $10,000 in cash and paychecks and $2,000 in future pay, money he hadn't even earned yet.

After ten years of abstinence, cold turkey, canceling bus trips to Atlantic City, as well as a flight to Vegas, after avoiding electronic poker machines and off-track betting, Mark thought he had his addiction beat. He'd even stopped looking through the sport's page in the morning paper, fearing that the temptation of the football or basketball spreads might lead him back to relapse.

*I had even given up sports for you!* he thought angrily, glancing at the sky. *Ten straight years, and this is how you thank me for making one slip?*

Mark hissed in disdain. Now this was a conundrum well beyond Hindu comprehension. He'd be going home soon, completely broke now, and far worse off than when he came; Mark could not remember a time in his life when he felt so out of control. Not only was his landlord waiting anxiously to be paid, but he was incurring an avalanche of personal debts as every day passed. Several of his credit cards were already maxed-out and his intent to pay them off slipped down the drain along with everything else. Indeed, he was beginning to feel genuinely lost in the forgotten hills and valleys of *Borabi;* and the longer he stayed the more psychologically drained he felt.

Mark, along with nearly 100 others, had already extended the stipulated term of their service contracts; but as far as Pendleton & Waxler was concerned, contract stipulations were mere technicalities for labor officials to pontificate back in the States. As long as there was work to be done along the Indian badlands, the construction company continued to test the flexibility of its own contracts.

Mark swept in toward a thicket of cactus brush and *Berrera* vines, deftly lowering the dozer's large mechanical clearing shovel; the Great Range of the Himalayan Mountains loomed skyward behind him, the frosted Matterhorn of Everest meandering up, its jagged precipices and cliffs a testament to its Ice-Age beginnings. Eventually disappearing into the clouds high above, Mount Everest was viewed as a blessing by the Eastern World, the glacier's activity bestowing countless fresh water streams, lakes, and rivers, the essentials for life.

On this late afternoon day visibility was excellent, and if he'd taken the time to look around Mark would have seen the multi-layered stratum of the mountain, its deciduous layer the darkest, near the bottom, before the lighter hue of the mountain's center where pines, conifers and firs abounded. And then there were the upper reaches of Everest, those between 18 and 28,000 feet, the harsh wasteland that gave this glacier its true meaning and significance.

But Mark was no longer impressed with the fabled monolith. He'd seen the mountain nearly every day for five solid months, and he was beginning to look right through this natural wonder. Indeed, the mountain and its history had lost its awesome appeal months ago.

After clearing several acres of field brush and bramble, Mark began clattering toward a gigantic willow stump in the center of a field. The two-hundred-year-old tree had towered nearly as many feet the day before, and now all that remained was its enormous stump and gnarled root system. The chainsaw teams had already been through here, and it was Mark's job to yank out the remains.

Before attacking the stump, Mark noticed that his K-411 tractor was getting low on fuel; the petroleum gauge was covered in dirt, but he could plainly see the fat red needle approaching Empty. He reached for the walkie-talkie atop the tractor's tool chest and contacted one of three fuel trucks catering to heavy equipment spread out over a 250 mile radius.

"I'm on the way Grid 16, " he heard a brusque voice reply.

Mark then tossed the radio aside and clattered toward the massive stump, raising his hydraulic shovel as he approached.

With a powerful surge, the large spade sank deep into the earth, wedging partially underneath the stump and nudging it slightly. After a second heavy "stab," Mark managed to rip loose the main anchor, but the rest of the root system remained tightly locked around a large outcropping of rock.

*A slab of granite,* thought Mark, fingering a red lever and withdrawing the giant shovel. *Or basalt.*

Like Sir Lancelot atop his spirited steed, Mark wheeled around to the other side, dozer tracks kicking up clouds of dirt, and again sent the hydraulic shovel slamming down.

Below him, the stump cracked in half, and for a moment he thought he could pry it loose in one great section. As a cloud of yellow-jackets began swarming wildly, Mark repositioned his "spade" for another heavy drop.

But his sustained efforts were utterly fruitless; after several minutes much of the tree above the surface had been torn away but, like a rotten tooth, the dying roots remained in tact. Realizing the futility, Mark again reached for his walkie-talkie.

"Jones! This is Black down at 16," he began irritably into the radio. A pair of yellow-jackets had found their way into his cabin, and Mark's hand began waving wildly. "I'm gonna need a few more charges placed down here. Fucking willow stump won't budge. Over."

There was no reply, and Mark repeated the message, only now adding: "…and bring some more hornet spray! You might need it more than me."

"Marko?" suddenly crackled a voice. "Where in the hell are you?"

"Up on Grid 16," replied the dozer operator, again swatting at a yellow-jacket dancing erratically near his face. "I'm waiting for fuel now, and I'm gonna need about ten pounds of the industrial heavy stuff. I found another Excalibur."

The reference to King Arthur's sword was indicative of the seemingly intractable nature of certain stumps which, much like the sword Excalibur, were purported to have been buried in stone. The construction lingo went on to include everything from a Pixie-Stick, which stood for a heavy crane, to Roach Coach, coming to represent the humble lunch wagons catering to the many construction workers.

"You're kidding, Marko!" hissed a voice through the tiny speaker. "My day is practically done! I was getting ready to head down to the Samsara Club for a beer. I'm meeting that little tramp from Calcutta. She'll be there with her sister tonight! Over!"

Mark rolled his eyes. The Samsara Club, a local watering hole established for the sole purpose of catering to the whims of American laborers, was one of three taverns owned and operated by Udo Enduto, a New Delhi entrepreneur with enough sense to realize the profits of such an operation. Udo was not alone in his logic. Along with the protracted construction endeavor eventually sprang a community, which quickly grew to a village and finally a 7,000 residential township. After all, someone was needed to run the laundry businesses, sell supplies, food, booze, and everything else a large team of construction workers would desire. Prostitution and drugs became vanguard markets but, since his relapse, Mark had decided to stop drinking and in no way desired the dark-skinned teenagers trying to win his affection for a few American dollars. Besides, he was flat broke.

"Why don't you leave that shovel and come join me?" pressed Jones. "Like I said, she's supposed to bring her sister!"

Mark sighed. Junior didn't seem to get it. The last thing he wanted to do was spend what little cash remained in his wallet on a drunken stupor, especially with Junior, one of the leaches that had bled him at the poker table. Besides, plying himself with alcohol would only sink him deeper into his depression.

"No thanks, Junior," replied Mark tiredly. "I like blondes. And I like them to be legal."

"Everything is legal here!" trumpeted Junior. "Got the Turkish cheese (a term for hashish) and the sweet teenage Honeys! This is better than the French Quarter on a Fat Tuesday! I'll lend you some money, and you can pay me back! I'll just add it onto your marker!"

Mark wiped a streak of grime from his face, and then felt a stinging near his shoulder. He swatted away a yellow-jacket that was humping his neck.

"Shit!" hissed Mark into the radio. "Do whatever you want, Junior! Where's Brinkman?"

A long sigh came through the radio. "We haven't seen him all day. Bonds said he had to run back to the States for a family emergency."

"Fine," replied Mark brusquely, rolling up an old, yellowed newspaper and swatting wildly at the second flying assailant. "But if Hickers comes around tomorrow and sees that stump sitting in an open field, somebody's head will roll, and it won't be mine!"

At the mention of Milton Hickers, Central Union's president and chief shareholder, there was a pause, and Jones' attitude changed:

*"Fine!"* hissed the demolition man. *"I'll be there when I get there! But don't hold your breath! Over and out!"*

Mark tossed the radio onto a tool box and became still and silent. A yellow-jacket had landed on the steering leaver of the dozer, its antennae moving like tiny wet noodles. Jack whacked at his flying nemesis, smashing the attacker with the yellowed sport's page of the *New York Times*. He then glanced at his watch. 3:31. The sun would begin setting in another hour; and just to the north another massive tangle of wilderness awaited him.

Mark felt a lance of frustration, raw impatience, and he could feel the very last straw bearing down on the camel's back. He wanted to redeem himself against this Excalibur, to blow off some steam in the process, to take five solid months of frustration out on this inanimate object.

He started the engine of his K-411 and leaned on the throttle. The tractor groaned and lurched forward, its exhaust pipe belching angry purple plumes. Mark engaged the right track and accelerated, simultaneously applying the brake to his left track. The braking system allowed one dozer track to remain stationary as the other turned, allowing the large vehicle to maneuver with relative ease. The sun began sinking low on the western horizon, the large hazy disk dipping into the tree line.

With a diesel roar, Mark surged ahead like a medieval knight, positioning his hydraulic arm like a jousting spear, the iron teeth of the shovel pointing straight down now. Mark dropped the heavy bucket, and a rolling "crack" filled the air. A large chunk of wood splintered and broke free, and the earth shifted under his treads.

As Mark jostled the mechanical arm deeper, a fuel truck came bouncing down the road, its driver signaling by flashing his headlights.

Mark never saw it. He again sank his giant shovel into the webbed root system, ripping loose both wood and soil. There was a hydraulic *hisss* as the tractor shrieked in protest and, with a flick of his fingers, Mark deftly withdrew the shovel and raised it high. He then drove it down with a violent surge; a loud crash rang out and the shovel sank beneath the stump. The dozer rocked wildly as Mark manipulated the arm, feeling like a dentist performing a large-scale root canal. There was suddenly a loud metallic screech, and the dozer itself was nearly flipped over by its own powerful arm. Mark immediately shut down the engine and clambered down from his seat. He jumped into the compost, construction boots mashing the ground as he hurried toward the stump.

"Fucking root system is unbelievable!" he roared, kicking at the stump.

"Get demolition over here," muttered the truck driver, slowly approaching the stump on foot. Larry Barnett had an unlit cigarette clenched between his teeth.

"Don't knock yourself out, Mark. Junior can blow that out in a jiffy."

Mark clambered onto the hood of the dozer and began studying the large hydraulic arm. "I know. I already called."

# 2

Junior Jones raced down the dirt trail like a rodeo bull on amphetamine, his 1998 Ford Expedition bucking wildly in a rocky culvert. Junior's fog lights were on High, his fat knobby tires were kicking up clouds of dust, and his rhino-liner was loaded with three cases of industrial dynamite.

As Jones wheeled past Grid 14 his headlights bounced along the dim path and lanced through the trees; he saw a fox dart across the road, a red-tail, before leaping into a bank of foliage and vanishing.

Junior didn't bother to brake. He knew these trails like he knew explosives: round and round, or so he thought. Junior was P&W's seasoned demolition's expert and had served a six-year tour of duty in the U.S. Army's Demolition Corps; as a result, he'd handled everything from C4 plastic to industrial dynamite. And at this stage of construction he was one of Pendleton & Waxler's busiest employees.

But Junior wasn't even scheduled to be on the clock tonight; and he didn't appreciate the sudden inconvenience.

Not one bit.

*Just wait till I get there,* Junior thought angrily, bouncing across a culvert. *I've got a big Nobel Peace Prize waiting for you, Blacky!*

The reference to Alfred Nobel, the creator of dynamite and, ironically enough, the originator of the Nobel Peace Prize, was a favorite of Junior's ironies.

"It's the Yin and Yang in all of us!" the veteran often purported.

*And tonight I'm going to open up a big can of Yang!*

As Junior navigated the undulating road with one hand on the steering wheel, his free hand deftly fingered the arming coil on a radio-controlled ignition box. It wasn't the safest method of triggering explosives, particularly with a maelstrom of other radio traffic in the area; but with the absence of overt interference, as well as other heavy equipment, it was a relatively safe exercise.

And despite his brazen exterior and acerbic disposition, Junior never played with fire.

After the nine-mile rodeo ride, Junior wheeled onto a smaller trail and disappeared behind a curtain of *Berrera*. Just ahead he could see the large Caterpillar being refueled; he could also see Mark and Belcher standing near the stump, hands stuffed inside their gray overalls.

Junior wheeled onto Grid 16 and came skidding to a stop, at least one hundred feet away from Mark and his tractor. His large knobby tires kicked up a cloud of dirt, and when the curtain cleared Junior was already out of the truck and walking toward Mark, his arms clutching a bundle of industrial dynamite.

Blasting was a bit more complicated than it initially appeared, at least to layman, perhaps even the journeyman, and Junior was privy to the many derivatives. Just as there were different pieces of heavy equipment for different duties, there were different types of explosives for different occasions. Formulas high in ammonium nitrate and including some sodium chloride were classified by the U.S. Bureau of Mines as "acceptable" for use in coal mines. Since they produced a flame that was strong yet brief, and cooled quickly enough so as to not ignite pockets of trapped methane, it brought down the risk of peripheral explosion, something every miner feared.

But the reasons were simple.

The intensity of a blast was determined by the nitroglycerin content. In the detonation process dynamite is converted to carbon dioxide, nitrogen dioxide, and water vapor. In coal mining or tunneling the presence of poisonous carbon monoxide and nitrogen dioxide is kept at a safe level by a careful balance of the ratio of nitrates and pulps in the grades intended for underground use. The burn rate determined by the mixture of these elements dictates the use for the explosives. Whether strip mining for coal, open pit mining of metal ores, or rock quarrying, other non-nitroglycerine blasting agents such as "water-gel" explosives, TNT, or powdered aluminum were preferred. If one's specialty happened to be building implosion or demolition, where steel girders, concrete and rebar needed to be displaced, small powerful plastic charges were used, along with a water gel ammonium nitrate.

When applying to open pit blasting, however, as was the case at hand, dynamite with high nitroglycerin and glycerin-ethylene was preferred. Stump demolition required the heavy stuff, explosives designed to create pressures exceeding one million pounds of pressure per square inch, enough force to lift Mark's dozer off its tracks.

"Hiya, Junior," began Mark, feeling a chord of discomfort returning. He and the bombastic demolition guru were not the best of friends. "I see you jumped on your pony and rode right over."

"No time for empty rhetoric," replied Junior hotly, walking past Mark and approaching the Excalibur. "Some of us with money are trying to get laid, and time's a wasting."

Tonight Junior wasn't mincing words. Carrying the bundles of dynamite, he disappeared beneath the stump and appeared about a minute later, scampering out of the hole, his pace noticeably quickened.

"We're gonna send this one to the moon," cajoled Junior, climbing into the dozer and looking down at Mark.

"Get in, and back the hell up."

Mark jumped into the driver's seat and flipped an orange ignition switch. The dozer grumbled to life. "How much did you plant down there?"

"Enough!" quipped Junior. "Now back up this beast!"

Mark rolled the tractor about fifty feet clear of the stump, and then turned toward it, raising the shovel for added protection.

"Why are you stopping here?" asked Junior.

"We're plenty clear," replied Mark, turning off the engine.

Junior shook his head from side to side. "Back it up another fifty. I planted so I wouldn't have to come back."

Not bothering to argue, Mark backed away another fifty feet and shut off the engine.

"There!" he exclaimed.

Junior nodded approvingly. He then began removing two small plastic caps, each affixed to the end of a copper wire. Junior didn't fool with conventional blasting caps and triggering devices; not if he didn't have to. He preferred triggering via radio waves, and the new Saturn Industrial Blasting Device worked like a charm.

Both men were gazing blankly through the Plexiglas windshield now, their eyes peering beneath the dozer shovel, which had become their insurance shield.

Junior always got a pleasurable grimace when detonating a charge and chuckled lightly before touching the wires.

A towering funnel of dirt and flying mulch suddenly appeared, and a bright flash of orange, the fiery nucleus. The thunderous roar came seconds later, a shockwave blowing across the dozer like the tail of a cyclone. The ground shook and the stump was launched into the air, tumbling end over end, before slowly whiffing down, a band of roots dangling wildly from its body. Both men winced as the enormous smoking cinder slammed onto the steel roof of the dozer, before tumbling heavily to the ground. For a moment neither man spoke; their ears were ringing. Mark then turned slowly toward Junior:

"Jeeze, Jones! How much did you pack it with?"

"Does it matter?" replied Junior, plucking a cigarette from a shirt pocket. "Your problem is solved."

All that remained of the willow stump was a crater where it had been firmly entrenched only seconds before.

But the thirty-five-year-old construction worker was about to encounter something altogether different; it was a dark portent of what was soon to come. And its enormous repercussions would leave the world forever changed.

As Junior returned to his truck and sped off the grid in a whirl of dust, Mark stepped cautiously toward the crater, as if uncertain that all the dynamite had detonated. He gazed down into the hole as a tourist may gaze into the mouth of Mount Kilauea, a curtain of smoke and sulfur whirling around him.

Barnett approached as well, a silly grin etched across his face. "Take the rest of the evening off, Black. I'd say Grid 16 is officially cleared."

Mark didn't respond. He was squinting into the mouth of the crater, unsure if he wasn't imagining things. He could see what looked like red patches of fabric, and then he saw what appeared to be some animal remains buried deep in the earth.

Mark climbed carefully into the hole, sliding knee-deep in dirt before reaching for the skull of a horse. The long bone was sticking awkwardly through the dirt. He then pulled at the sleeve of a uniform, and the waterlogged fabric nearly disintegrated between his fingers. Although the tunic separated to his touch, he reached for an old leather strap with a canteen attached.

"What you got there, Mark?" asked Barnett.

"I don't know," replied Black.

"Probably animal bones," began Barnett, finally lighting the cigarette. "No telling what's buried out here."

Then, Barnett's eyes narrowed. "Look, I see something else!"

Mark turned and saw the thick bones, which he mistook for a horse's hind quarters. The remains were dense, thick and heavy.

As Mark continued his haphazard excavation he discovered the breach of an old canon sticking through the mud, and part of a wooden wheel missing several spokes.

Then he saw something very disturbing. When Mark yanked the frightful object from the wall of dirt, he wasn't sure if he should drop it and start running, or toss it up to Belcher. He could see the ear hole and what looked like a nasal cavity; but when he turned the skull around he was startled to see a gnarly row of pointed teeth smiling back. Mark's mind raced with visions of a giant gorilla or baboon.

Deciding to keep the unusual bone, Mark began walking up the wall of the crater. It was harder going up, and he suddenly lost his footing, dropping the heavy skull which tumbled back into the hole. Mark turned to reach for his trophy, but his boots sank into the dirt and an avalanche of clay came rolling down.

Along with a charnel of grueling remains.

A wave of uniformed skeletons began tumbling through the wall of dirt, falling around Mark Black as if clattering a dark caveat.

# 3

As the dish of the sun dipped below the sierra of the Himalayas, casting a deep orange hue along the rusting 32' trailer, a wild llama sauntered cautiously out of the brush, its wet nose sniffing the air. The animal strolled toward a trashcan behind the trailer and began picking through paper wrappings and discarded fruit rinds. The trailer, strategically hidden behind a copse of *Berrera* vines, was invisible to traffic along the main road to Delhi.

Inside the portable office file cabinets loomed in the shadows, a thick padlock for every drawer, and a metal desk was situated against one wall, its top cluttered with research papers, an old microscope, and a metal crucible with an attached Bunsen burner. Stacks of books littered the floor with titles such as *The First Tower of London; William the Conqueror; 73 A.D.: Herod the Great; Western Asia Under Alexander; The Andean Culture; Homer And The Fall of Troy; The Bronze Age;* and *Mahayana Buddhism.*

From the back bedroom, which had been converted to additional office space, a radio scanner occasionally hissed and popped, the voices of construction workers reverberating through the aluminum shell. As the scanner again crackled to life with a staccato of warbled voices, a young woman entered the trailer and went to her desk. She clicked on a lamp and pulled up a swivel chair, before crossing her long legs.

Tatiana Borosky was tall and well-tanned, and today she wasn't wearing a bra; her ample breasts jiggled freely, their nipples occasionally standing at attention beneath the extra-large T-shirt. Her strawberry blonde hair was pulled back in a tight bun, and although she'd gotten very little sleep the past few days her green eyes possessed an intense, intelligent quality.

Tatiana shifted uncomfortably in the chair and began to gently unwrap a piece of cheese cloth. As she untied a section of twine, the thermostat "clicked" on and she heard the hissing of gas feeding the propane heater. Although Tatiana had made due with the cramped quarters, she would have

29

preferred a stationary tenement near New Delhi to conduct her ongoing research.

But the trailer was mobile, and mobility was an essential factor on this prodigious "dig."

Her "office" had been parked outside Grid 21 for the past two weeks, and as she removed a bone fragment from the cloth, peering at its contours through a magnifying glass, she listened intently to the radio scanner which again hissed and crackled from the adjoining room. Intercepting the voices of Pendleton & Waxler employees had proven highly advantageous on this particular assignment, providing the scholar with valuable firsthand information along the entire length of the dig. And Tatiana was not positioned in this section of brush by accident. For the past two years the Ukrainian researcher had followed the various construction units. Her research had initially centered on the ancient Hittite culture which had eventually assimilated into the Indus Valley nearly two-thousand years ago.

But as her work unfolded Tatiana began to recognize an even larger theses evolving, something so incredible that the dissertation itself no longer held importance.

And as the American construction teams continued peeling away large tracts of forest, she could feel the inevitable drawing closer, closer than ever, and she began to feel like an Argonaut closing in on the Golden Fleece.

The bone she studied was highly unusual. It was recovered from Grid 13 when the dozers began clearing the fringe of jungle near *Alcuoco*. She'd heard them talking over the radio about uncovering what appeared to be a mass grave, and when she hurried to the site Tatiana discovered a plethora of human remains as well as fifteen "highly unusual" artifacts pertinent to her research.

*Bone density unlike anything I've ever seen*, she thought, glaring down into the black marrow. She estimated that the fragment was between two and three-hundred years old. She'd found some much older, with the very same unusual configuration. And that's what baffled her. Whatever was living out here was unknown to modern evolution. And by the looks of it, they'd been here longer than anyone could have imagined.

*And the jungle is their cover,* she thought with a rising sense of enchantment.

A clay tablet, discovered by Tatiana in the Indus Valley, told some of the enigmatic story. The prophesy was scribbled in Aramaic, and after consulting a well-known etymologist from Frankfurt, Germany, Tatiana learned of the dark caveats contained therein. The hieroglyphic scribble mentioned an ornate sacrificial site located somewhere in the mountains, a religious site where the gatekeepers were "appeased with the blood of peasants and criminals."

But more important than the site were the creature deities which engendered such reverence and fear. Little became known of the Hittites after they vanished from the pages of ancient scripture, and it now appeared that Tatiana was about to fully understand their secret Diaspora into India.

The Ukrainian anthropologist reached for another artifact, a human femur bone, and again peered intently through the magnifying glass. The bones were just like the others. Covered in deep scratches, as if caught in a human masticator, the lashes and lacerations were deeply embedded in the bone, and several specimens had been severed clean to the core, exposing the black gleam of petrified marrow.

But before Tatiana could scrutinize the artifact any further, the scanner crackled to life and her eyes went wide.

"Hey Hollinger, this is Black up on 16. I found some really weird shit over here and we may want someone to have a look at this. Something doesn't look right. I found a canon also, and a musket."

# 4

Tatiana was there within the hour, racing recklessly across the bumpy flatlands, her AMC Jeep loaded high with rolls of tent canvass, shovels, coolers, rope, lanterns, and a cache of other hand tools. Much of the Jeep was covered in rust, and a pattern of scratches and dings ambled along its dented body. With its mud-caked wheel-wells and filthy windshield, the vehicle looked as if it had been resurrected from the underbrush of *Borabi* itself. A wooden crucifix dangled erratically from the rear-view mirror, and a faded bumper-sticker on the trailer hitch read: "Better Dead Than Red!"

Having been born and raised in Communist Ukraine, and having lived the first fifteen years of life under the hammer and sickle, Tatiana had no trouble expressing her revulsion for her Bolshevik "captors." It had been a very dark and mundane childhood existence. She remembered that her father had been forced to work for the military establishment, and that her mother was employed at a textile factory in the heart of Kiev. Due to inferior medical and sanitary conditions, her younger brother Hugo had died of tuberculosis when he was only five years old.

And that was all she needed to remember.

"Communism is slavery, pure and simple!" she had proclaimed the day Lech Walesa took his stand for Solidarity in Poland. And although she began to freely express opinion long-considered criminal by the State, Tatiana knew she spoke for the silent majority of Ukrainians. Since her life had been a dreary trek through mediocrity, through concrete apartment buildings and chain-link fences, the Warsaw-Pact leaders steadfastly cruel and indifferent, Tatiana was left with a deep disdain for the travesty known as Stalinist Russia. Since the memories of her homeland, as well as her childhood, were often blurred and opaque, without passion, detail or clarity, she felt a deep resolution to make the necessary transition to a capitalistic world. Free markets, equal opportunity and civil liberties were foreign and exotic concepts to Tatiana. And as she threw herself into her work she vowed to remain focused on the American Dream, a distant concept that sidled closer with every passing day.

And she would not waste another precious second fulfilling that dream.

Within minutes after arriving at Grid 16, Tatiana had the excavation site cordoned off, and a string of lanterns were glowing bright. A generator chugged methodically in the moonlight, and the sexy anthropologist began making quick notations in a spiral ledger.

Mark studied the attractive post-graduate from his tractor, his mind filling with an avalanche of questions. Out here in the jungle, at night, there was something mysterious and captivating about the inquisitive foreign scientist. Mark began to think of a 1980s *Raiders of the Lost Ark* movie.

As Tatiana jumped into the crater, sliding down to the mass of bones, Mark lit a cigarette and climbed down from the K-411. Without a word Tatiana began digging dirt away from the horse's twisted remains, her gloved hands careful and deft.

"I think it is safe to assume that this horse was towing that cannon when it died," she said assuredly.

Although her Slavic accent was very pronounced, Tatiana was careful to articulate every word with exacting emphasis. Yet her choppy American syntax, splashed with the slurry of her Ukrainian tongue, had a melodious chirp to it. Mark found her tone and vernacular very appealing.

Kind of sexy.

"The cannon is British," she continued with a ring of expertise. "Probably built during the 1700s. The barrel is smooth-bore, which means it is of the antebellum war era. Rifling did not occur until the middle of the 17th Century. This is indeed very old."

Tatiana wasn't only schooled in anthropology; her minors included archaeology and geology, and in 2008 she graduated from the University of Kiev near the top of her class, receiving her Master's Degree *summa cum laude.* The university's Sciences Department was sorry to see her go, but nothing could contain the aspiring scientist, now free of the socialist yoke and determined to throw herself into her new profession as she battled toward her doctorate.

Tatiana immediately lost interest in the old piece of artillery and began glaring at the heap of uniformed bones, notably the many deep scratches along the skeletons. Some of the osteo-lacerations were so deep that the bone had nearly been severed in half. She was certain they were bite marks, and she was convinced that she was on the verge proving her abstract scientific theory.

Tatiana then turned and noticed Mark staring down, his handsome silhouette created by the lanterns. Suddenly feeling self-conscious, she smiled. She was being totally self-absorbed again.

"I was once digging at the base of K2," she began softly. "I was searching for a Hittite sacrificial site, and soon discovered an entire charnel of animal bones. I was initially very excited since I was preparing to complete my dissertation on the Hittite migration."

Tatiana paused and drew a deep breath.

"But I discovered that the bones were from an 18th Century Hindu restaurant in Calcutta. It was such a disappointment."

Mark chuckled, glancing back down at the human remains.

"I have a feeling that's not the case here."

Tatiana forced a smile.

No, it wasn't. She was certain of that.

Tatiana's assistant, Ahmel Stabba, suddenly appeared. The Egyptian foreign exchange student jumped into the hole and worked in silence. The olive-skinned North African began wrapping the horse bones in sheets of burlap, tying off the specimens with rope before recording the information in an archaeological logbook.

Mark felt a stab of envy, and struggled to think of something to say.

"How long will it take you to get what you need?" began the heavy equipment operator. "I was supposed to be finished this grid by nightfall. It looks like I'll have to come back tomorrow."

"Just a few hours," replied Tatiana instantly. "By tomorrow morning we should have everything we need. After we collect the smaller artifacts, we will be removing the cannon with my Jeep. I have a winch attached."

Mark nodded and glanced at his watch. He knew he could simply resume his clearing on Grid 17, but wanted to find out more about this beautiful woman, this person who effortlessly filled him with such intrigue.

In no hurry to return to his tent, Mark took a seat in the dirt at the mouth of the hole.

"I've got something in my tractor you may want to look at," began Mark calmly, hoping that Ahmel wasn't her lover as well as her assistant.

"I'd love to see it," replied Tatiana, not bothering to look up.

Tatiana's eyes were sweeping slowly across every inch of the crater, before suddenly stopping. The short, thick sternum was caked with red clay, but she could see the grotesque outline in the mud. As she began pushing away the dirt, another bone appeared, and then a convoluted skeletal assembly was poking grotesquely through the wall of dirt. A mandible appeared, packed with mud and red clay, and she stared in wonderment at the gnarled row of pointed teeth, which resembled those of a killer whale. Tatiana noticed that the appendages appeared to be simian, but the hipbone indicated a bipedal configuration, something she'd long suspected. Her heart began racing.

"Ahmel! Down here! Hurry!"

The assistant jumped back into the hole and began digging through the dirt with both hands, his eyes wide with amazement. They unearthed another torn piece of red fabric, and as Tatiana held it up into the fading light, Mark realized it had been a uniform of some sort. He could see red tassels and brass buttons.

"Collect and tag the thorax and spinal column," she said intensely, scampering out of the hole and returning to her Jeep. "And then start excavating the western wall!" she shouted to Ahmel. "We don't have much time!"

Mark went to his tractor and grabbed the frightful skull from atop his tool chest. He knew the archaeologist would get a real kick out of it.

As Tatiana continued rummaging frantically through the back of her Jeep, Mark sauntered up behind her, carrying the heavy artifact like a large Halloween pumpkin.

"Look what I found," he said casually, extending the skull toward her.

Tatiana turned, and her mouth fell agape. She dropped her notebook and sheets of paper fluttered in the wind.

Tatiana seemed frozen in time.

"Oh my God!" she finally stammered.

# 5

The sun was rising when she finally made it back to her office; but Tatiana was far from finished the excavation, and not the least bit tired. Even before Ahmel could stack the specimens atop the examination table, Tatiana was unwrapping the burlap "packages," eager to begin the tedious task of re-assembling the many fragments of bone. The British canon remained outside the trailer, wrapped in a green tarpaulin. But it was the very last thing on her mind.

In just under seven hours they'd recovered eight full human skeletons, remains of men belonging to a military unit of a distant era.

But they'd found something else, and Tatiana had difficulty containing her enthusiasm. She must remain calm,  at least until the skeletal remains were fully assembled; and although she didn't voice her lofty expectations, she knew she was on the verge of something comparable to discovering a living fossil.

*But bigger!* she reminded herself. *Much, much bigger!*

The facts began to dictate the truly incredible. And the more she learned, the more she began to identify the fascinating and frightful reality. Whatever was happening here was beyond human comprehension, beyond the localized evolutionary laws of planet Earth.

To this point Tatiana had collected only scattered and incomplete sets of bones: a fibula here, two tibias and a partial ribcage there. But she already knew that the remains belonged to an animal unknown to modern Science, an animal familiar only to the ancient Hittites.

And as the "big dig" continued, the middle-aged Ukrainian geologist completely forgot about her Hittite dissertation, entitled "Cursed People In A Cursed Land." The thesis would have been well-documented and choked with detailed exposition and corroborating facts; but as she stroked the large, mud-caked cranial cavity, she looked like a young girl on Christmas

Morning. Tatiana might as well have been opening a gift-wrapped Barbie doll.

*It will take an act of India's congress to stop me now!* she thought excitedly, removing clay from the unusual eye sockets. But it was, after all, the Indian Government that provided her funding through a number of grants, and Tatiana was well aware of their immense commitment to this rail project. She didn't want to do anything which may appear as a threat to that project. Besides, she didn't want to make any waves for Artonus.

Artonus Rozpaz.

She'd met the parliamentary representative while applying for one of the many *Borabi* grants being offered to the public. But Tatiana was not a citizen of India, and Artonus would find a way to make her eligible, nonetheless. In him, Tatiana found a robust lover and an essential connection; but little else.

Artonus was not her type.

And as Tatiana slipped the missing mandible into place, Artonus slipped from her mind. She was looking at the incredible.

Tatiana was convinced that the human race was enduring an ongoing cycle of evolution. We were growing into our brains. There were other modifications, losing our hair, the non-essential existence of our appendix, and an ever-expanding cranial cavity assured her that the human race was continuing to experience evolution and the miracle of adaptation.

But whatever she was looking at had evolved into a monstrosity.

And Tatiana was convinced that it had *not* taken place on Earth.

# 6
# Grid 29

The Ganges River cut a meandering green swath through the jungle of *Borabi* like a gnarled tract of winding *Berrera*. At the river's delta the currents were shallow and widely dispersed and the fresh water eased gently into the Bay of Bengal. But as the river wound through *Borabi*, 200 miles further south, the waters raged through the jungle in a narrow vortex, a concentrated funnel of deep water, and powerful, sweeping currents. The Ganges was its most narrow here, a whirling bottleneck that swelled from its banks from melting snow in spring, as well as the heavy rains of summer.

But Milton Hickers had already taken that into account.

And so had his engineers.

As the cigarette boat chugged up the river from the south, inboard engines blubbering rudely, Milton took a seat on the fiberglass engine mount, his eyes combing through the tall banks of red mud flanking him on either side.

It would be his most challenging operation yet.

After the boat chugged another hundred yards, the pilot flipped the throttle killed the engines. As Milton's assistant hurled an anchor into the murky waters, the cigarette drifted swiftly in the currents, its fiberglass hull slapping the horizontal swells.

"This is it," grumbled Frank Torelli, removing his sunglasses and stretching. "I think it's the best spot."

Milton Hickers nodded, but his eyes were transfixed to an outcropping of granite near the shoreline.

*It's the only spot,* thought Milton.

The freight magnet immediately began to visualize the wooden trusses that would one day reach out through the tangle of trees, before spanning three hundred meters across the fierce waterway. The concrete reinforcement pylons, bracing the railroad bridge for heavy freight as well as light passenger trains, were currently being cast at the *Varanasi* rock yard, and were already scheduled to be lowered into place with heavy cranes.

*It's just as Anthony Hall had predicted,* thought Milton with a chord of optimism. *Considering the tunnel's proximity, just thirty miles to the east, it's the only feasible spot.*

"Hall says there won't be any problem running the generator recoil along the riverbed," began Torelli, motioning to the rushing water. "And the fiber optics will go right along next to them, as well as the main transitory feed line."

Torelli was leaning on the freeboard of the sleek boat, chewing on the nub of a cigar. The thickset Italian had been with Milton from the beginning, when Central Union was a modest track supplier to the big companies. And, due to his union connections, Tony wielded nearly as much power as Milton himself, especially considering his relationship with Ralphie Morano, an influential Teamster spokesman.

"Just how is Lechler supposed to get his trucks down here?" blathered Milton, playing the traditional role of devil's advocate. His thin, bony hand was shielding the sun from his eyes. "We couldn't drive down here ourselves."

"Milt, I can have a trail opened in one week," replied Torelli confidently. "Three Caterpillars, seven days."

Milton nodded, but didn't respond. Torelli would know. Not only did the big Italian maintain close ties with the heavy equipment firms, he'd worked with many of these very same men in building the new and enormous Casino Park near Portland, Maine. The multi-hotel contract, which included parking garages as well as a new network of roads, was completed in six years, and when Hickers finally lured the ambitious contractor back to Central Union, he put him right to the big test.

That's how Milton worked. The 72 year old railroad tycoon rarely accepted "No" for an answer, and his sole purpose in life was to act in the name of Progress, of Capital, and of Eminent Domain. Whether it be a tie-tracks around Lake Victoria, or several hundred miles of ribbon through the Sudan, if it could at all be accomplished, Milton would see it that it was.

But before he could vocalize his thoughts, Torelli's cellular phone began chirping.

The big Italian snatched the Motorola off his belt and pressed a button.

"Torelli here."

After a few seconds he said, "He's not available right now. What's the problem?"

After a moment of silence, Torelli added, "I'll tell him when I see him." Then he hung up.

"They're barking again, Milton," said Torelli evenly.

"Let me guess," replied Milton. "The tunnel?"

Torelli nodded. "We may want to get back and find out what's going on."

Milton Hickers agreed, and Torelli fingered the ignition switch; the cigarette's engines grumbled to life. As Torelli turned the boat around and leaned on the accelerator, Milton gazed at the tree line.

He already knew what their problem was.

# 7

The blueprints were situated atop an enormous table of volcanic rock, spread out like a map of the Eastern Front. As the sun crested gently over the sprawling hills of the Himalayan valley, eight men stood at the piedmont of the great mountain; but they were not chatting merrily in the mild breeze, something they'd done two months earlier.

The architects and engineers of Central Pacific Railroad and Pendleton & Waxler Construction were discussing the most enterprising and controversial stretch of track in the world.

Architects with the Montana-based railroad had already been over the detailed drawings numerous times; but they'd grown at odds with P&W engineers who remained convinced that the chosen site was the best alternative to crossing *Borabi*. Especially now. They were already encountering a significant structural deterioration within the tunnel, and the exhaust from the many concrete trucks and heavy equipment, particularly the new P&W Razorbacks, were nearly overwhelming the circulatory air pumps. It was becoming a double-edged quagmire, and the engineers remained staunchly divided in their views.

But each of the opinions were valued. Many of these men had already made their mark with Central Pacific Railroad overseas, laying nearly four-thousand miles of track throughout sub-Sahara Africa and along its eastern coast. The Montana railroad had chiseled through the Congo, around the southern portion of Lake Victoria, and had even laid nearly six-hundred miles through the Sahara desert, connecting a freight line from Sudan to Ethiopia. The 67-year-old company was awarded this assignment for that very reason: India's upper and lower houses of parliament were appreciative of their efforts in these Second and Third World endeavors.

But all of the altruistic hype was gone now.

Anthony Hall was studying the blueprints as Michelangelo might appraise the ceiling of the Sistine Chapel. The chief electrician followed the power lines through the main circuit board on the blueprints, adamant that his work not go to waste. Next to him, Patrick Lechler, the concrete foreman, waited patiently for the decision concerning ongoing construction of the tunnel. Just to the southwest was the gravel pit where his crews were expected to mix, pour, set and finish six million metric yards of concrete.

But all of his men were suddenly placed on stand-bye.

Anthony Hall, a structural engineer from the Bronx New York, wasn't in the mood for another debate. Anthony was a graduate of Texas Technical Institute, entering his profession at a time when engineering technology and understanding was changing gears, when lead pipes gave way to PVC, when semi-conductors replaced magnets, when satellites replaced spy planes and radio towers.

As a result, he'd gotten the best of both worlds, and few contested his blueprints or mathematical logic.

Until now.

Lechler was leaning on the hood of his Ford Explorer, shouting up to the others who were standing on the platform of rock. Just ahead of him, two logging rigs rumbled out of the forest, giant clouds of dust and sand whipping through the air.

"Besides, the leeway track needs to be raised!" continued Lechler hotly, his eyes rolling across the group of men. "After you make the turn on the north end, the inner convex of granite becomes too narrow!"

The design engineer smiled. It was getting late and now this overpaid laborer suddenly wanted to become a physicist.

"And those caves and caverns are going to create immeasurable structural problems," continued the concrete foreman. "We have no idea of their extent of breadth."

"Those caverns are aberrations!" barked the chief electrician. "You don't even know the extent of those caves!"

"That's exactly my point!" growled the foreman. "And neither do you!"

The electrician didn't reply; he merely scowled and glanced back at the blueprints.

In the distance came a roll of thunder as another charge of dynamite was detonated.

Carl McCaffery, a mid-level electrician from Jacksonville, Florida, continued to listen with an air of disinterest. The young technical advisor's mind began drifting away from the fragile platform of human engineering, and began ambling across the process of mountain making, God's supreme form of engineering. As the opposing firms pressed the debate of tunnel feasibility, Carl's mind drifted to the process of mountain-making, God's supreme form of engineering. Carl knew that, even as they spoke, immense forces were shifting under their very own feet. The electrician distinctly remembered the Voltair-Buffon argument concerning the discovery of ancient sea shells atop K2 and several other mountaintops. He also knew that the shape of the Earth was in a constant flux, and that they were currently standing on crust no more than forty miles thick. Then there was the mantle, conveying lava and molten nickel from the fiery core to the surface in an ongoing process of cooling.

And the deeper you got, the hotter it became.

Carl's eyes again drifted to the crested divisions of the mountain range, protruding skyward like an enormous saw blade. The adjoining basin was equally rugged. Ironically, the resultant culverts, called moraines, provided the optimum track platform, making it seem almost natural that a train should run through here. The patterns of rock left behind as the ice melted, organized rows of stone as it flowed away, was magnificent and beautiful, and the many passengers destined to ride the Orient Express II would see these magnificent moraines of stratified rock, the glacial build-up along the edge of a moving glacier. And the culverts of stone, resultant from the shifting tectonic plates, would also provide the perfect platform.

Carl then remembered that it was also very important not to clear the forested slopes, as the bristling hills acted as a preventive measure to recurring mudslides. But in some areas foliage was altogether nonexistent, precipitating the installation of makeshift 'ladders' of fencing along the steep inclines, a manmade form of avalanche prevention.

Carl's thoughts were suddenly scattered when he heard the scratchy voice of Junior Jones crackling over the short-wave radio.

"We have a minor delay on 16, Camp. It should be taken care of by early afternoon."

Now Milton Hickers, president and chief shareholder, flashed angry eyes as he reached for the radio.

"What kind of delay?" burst the rail magnate.

"They found more bones or something," continued Jones. "Looks like the remnants of something British. We have a local geologist up there now. We don't want to accidentally desecrate the place. Bad PR. She's been authorized to collect some bones and will be gone in the next couple of hours. Over."

"Make sure she is!" barked Milton into the radio. "I don't want to start sliding behind schedule. Lechler is getting ready to come through there. Over!"

Milton tossed the radio aside and turned his gaze back to the men surrounding the blueprints. He didn't like the way things were beginning to look. They now seemed to be unearthing a mass grave at almost every grid; and people were beginning to talk.

Another blast suddenly echoed through the valley.

"How are you going to compensate," hissed the concrete foreman, bringing the discussion back to the tunnel and its iniquities. "The north corner alone will be a genuine trouble spot. I can't believe you won't acknowledge that simple reality!"

The tunnel curled at a 45-degree angle, and the maximum height and width needed to accommodate the largest of freight trains was under scrutiny. "I know it's not going to be a daily, or even yearly occurrence, but the southbound connector and the northbound express are going to pass one another in that tunnel. You can't deny that it's going to happen from time to time throughout rail operations!"

Carl decided to listen. The concrete foreman made a solid argument. The new M-105 locomotives were indeed enormous machines, each over one-hundred feet long and nearly ten-feet wide. But Carl could also understand the railroad's position. Abandoning the tunnel now would mean the construction of another bridge, one larger than any of the other three that were currently under construction. It would mean laying nearly four-hundred miles of additional track, something that was certain to bog down the current projected time tables, while hitting Central Pacific right in the pocketbook.

And Milton Hickers, listening to the debate with a twisted scowl, didn't even want to consider that bleak possibility.

"Forget about those caves!" flared Hickers. "I want to check the width and angle of that tunnel right this minute!"

# 8

As another tube of blueprints were unfurled, Milton drew a deep breath and hissed aloud. Although the project was only entering its second year, Central Pacific Railroad had already bored seven miles into the Himalayan mountain range and was expected to complete the tunneling at least two years ahead of schedule. It was a prodigious beginning, and was made possible in part by the P&W Razorback, a diesel-powered tractor with a large circular drilling bush mounted to its chassis. Essentially, it was a tractor with a steel porcupine attached, a high speed circulating bush designed to remove dirt and rock without the detrimental structural issues surrounding the abundant use of dynamite. Used in conjunction with measured amounts of blasting, the Razorbacks became an integral part of the railroad's tunneling project. And it was due to this unusual machine that Pendleton & Waxler remained well ahead of their projected timetables.

Something imperative to the project's financial feasibility.

*And we have come too far to stop now,* thought Milton.

As special trucks began lowering quarter-mile lengths of ribbon track, a large leap over the traditional and cheaper tie-tracks, tunnel excavation began in earnest, with a twenty-two-mile subterranean tube planned to run through a small corner of the Himalayan basin. A concrete culvert had already been poured along the adjoining moraines, and the ribbon track had been unfurled in long, thick ropes. The enormous steel coils of rail were expensive, and the first of its kind to be used in India.

But laying twenty-two miles of track was just a small part of the enormous operation. The Trans-East Rail Company, owned and operated by the Indian government, had itself set forth a similar proposal before realizing they would need help, and lots of it. And when the project took shape, there would be ten other companies involved with the enormous "dig," and six of those were American-based.

Entire forests needed to be cleared, before an 1,855-mile concrete culvert was cut, poured, and finished. This required an operation surpassing the Hoover Dam in scope and breadth. And at *Honchura*, along the Nepal/Indian border, a gigantic rail-yard was already under construction, replete with cranes, a trucking depot and multiple warehouses.

But clearing underbrush and pouring concrete was one thing; tunneling through twenty-two miles of rock had never been remotely endeavored. This wasn't a mine shaft; modern railroad tunneling was an altogether different task. Although explosives were used to begin the work of both, special care and structural considerations needed to be addressed in tunneling. Geological teams were required to search for everything from hidden fault lines to underground caves, issues that could doom a tunnel from the very beginning. Choosing the path of least resistance was the goal, erstwhile accounting for a voluminous compendium of structural issues and considerations.

Everything from the amount and type of explosives used, to the overhead embrasures assured that tunneling would remain a precise science. And although the railroad would be freight oriented, it was expected to draw tourists and travelers from around the world as well. And since the railroad was designed to link four eastern countries (India, Nepal, Tibet, China), nobility and citizen alike would soon be able to experience the East from an American designed rail system.

It would be the East's answer for the Autobahn.

Although the entire railroad would take nearly twelve years to complete, it was expected to exemplify American industrial ingenuity, equaling the Chunnel, Europe's aquatic tunnel linking Britain to the mainland; and concerning earth removal, the Orient Express II, something coined by Milton Hickers himself, was expected to displace ten times more dirt and rock than Boston's Big Dig. The operation was groundbreaking, in more ways than one.

The Orient Express II would ultimately link New Delhi with Peking, opening the Eastern world to new avenues of commerce and trade, the fruits of cooperation and political détente.

Yet the controversial tunnel remained Pendleton & Waxler's main concern. This was not a simple mining shaft; this was an enormous portal expected to accommodate two enormous locomotives as they passed one another in darkness. It would be the first time India, Pakistan, China, Nepal and Tibet worked cooperatively on a single endeavor together. Ever.

And due to their heightened diplomatic awareness, the former enemies and religious foes would be awarded the greatest of national gifts: a freight-line through the Himalayas.

As far as Milton Hickers was concerned, this was the opportunity every industrial entrepreneur could only dream of. Considered a shrewd opportunist even in his kinder, gentler days, Milton's altruistic appearance was merely skin deep, a mirage in the sand. Hickers was a business man, pure and simple, and he'd known, from the very beginning, that his growing company was too small to compete with the bigger domestic railroads, namely Union Pacific and American Freight. As a means of survival Milton began looking for greener pastures, which happened to be along the   East-African basin. And after twenty-five years of grim determination, the labors and sacrifice had finally paid off, landing him the most historic contract in the history of railroads.

Milton became determined to diminish the efforts of the American railroad icon Henry Morrison Flagler, and every developmental phase of his project was vigorously developed and employed.

Indeed, the entire Middle East, notably Pakistan and Afghanistan, as well as every other nation bordering and including China and India, would ultimately reap the benefits of the Orient Express II. And everything from oil headed to China, AK-47s bound for Pakistan, VCRs going to India, or textiles going to Afghanistan, *Everything* would be subjected to tolls and excise taxes, of which Central Pacific would receive a percentage, assuring that, upon completion, the American railroad would remain forever in the fiscal black.

But *until* that tunnel was finished, everything would remain theory.

And Milton Hickers was determined to make it a reality.

His reality.

As an engineer from Central Pacific Railroad approached the table of rock, opening a long cardboard tube and pulling out yet another roll of parchment, Milton stood.

Unfurled before him was a detailed map of the controversial tunnel, its hearty power grid detailed in blue ink.

"Let's take it from the top!" bellowed Milton Hickers as another blast echoed through the valley.

# 9
# Memorial Day
# Washington D.C.

Security was at a premium.

As the Nation's Capitol reveled in the holiday's fanfare and festivities, which was to later include a brilliant fireworks display near the Washington Monument, an air of merriment and reverie continued to emanate from Independence Drive all the way up to Pennsylvania Avenue. The Memorial Day parade was an enormous draw, with over five-hundred groups participating and numerous floats bobbing along the wide D.C. avenues.

As the District of Columbia Fire Department paraded across Washington Drive with a hook and ladder, the AFLAC duck towered above the Jefferson Memorial, and the Met-Life Snoopy was close behind, undulating from side to side above Lincoln Park. The Towson University marching band appeared at 14th Street and Constitution Avenue, lean drum majorettes twirling batons as they marched down flowering rows of cherry blossoms. District Mayor Melvin Tomlinson put in an appearance as well, riding in a 2010 convertible Ford Mustang, he and his young wife waving enthusiastically at the many people thronging along the thoroughfare. Then came the Morgan State Golden Bears, four sinuous rows of green and white, trumpets blaring and drummers sending their thunderous beat across half of the District.

There was great activity in the air as well.

Not only were additional F-16s deployed from Shaw Air Force Base, but the Blue Angels were scheduled for a ceremonial fly-over; and gradually descending from 20,000 feet was the President's private helicopter.

Air Force One dropped from a cloudbank in Virginia and began closing on the Potomac River at two-hundred mph, its aluminum skin shining bright in the summer sun. The President's aerial "limousine" had just received Israeli Prime Minister Aaron Sheltori at Andrews Air Force Base, and was scheduled to deliver him onto the White House lawn for what the President called, "Another solid measure in the recipe for peace and prosperity throughout the Middle-East."

But for much of the day, the President could not be found at the Pennsylvania Avenue tenement.

The Commander-In-Chief was across the river in Arlington, Virginia, standing reverently before the Tomb Of The Unknown Soldier. Just beneath the 50-ton marble cenotaph were the remains of an anonymous American soldier who, as the sarcophagus read, was, "…Known But To God."

As a sentinel from The Old Guard continued the eternal march of reverence, the U.S. Marine Corps' Honor Guard began their routine, bolt-action rifles spinning in perfect unison. Their exercise was fluent and crisp, and their white caps seemed to glow in the afternoon sun. Much of the President's cabinet was in attendance, as well. The Secretary of Defense, Melvin Knoll, stood next to the undersecretary, his customary scowl recognized by all; and in the back row was the Secretary of Labor, Anthony Watson, as well as the new National Security Advisor, Adam Kensington.

Contessa Brice again glanced toward the stone monument. As the Marine Corps drummers began the solemn roll of *Taps,* the Blue Angels appeared overhead. The squadron of F-18 Hornets were flying in their familiar "missing-man" formation, with an open slot representing the missing right wing man.

The lost soldier.

After the Blue Angels pulled away, there was a moment of silence. Contessa Brice then turned to a master sergeant dressed in Marine blues and threw a quick, firm salute. The military figure returned the formal greeting and spun on a heal. He then barked an order.

A Twenty-One-Gun-Salute was executed, cracking aloud in the mid-afternoon sun. The seven Marine Honor Guards reloaded in unison, before taking aim again. A second unified crack filled the air. After a third honorary salvo, the guard marched to the rostrum and stood at attention. The master sergeant rifled a salute and the President returned it.

Then the Speaker of the House, Harold Philbin, approached a cluster of microphones atop the stage.

"Ladies and Gentlemen, the President of the United States."

Everyone stood and a wave of applause rolled through the air.

Some said her beauty was classical, a Betty Davis gaze combined with the soft sorrel features of Cleopatra. Her distinguished cheekbones were set apart by intelligent brown eyes, and her smooth, easy gait reflected a level of sound fitness. But many political analysts said it was her dimpled smile that had won her the election, a smile best described by *Time* Magazine as a "…childlike simper, innocent and pure."

President Brice waited graciously as the applause continued, rising in crescendo for several long minutes. The popular president smiled brightly as her many constituents extolled their praises of support affection.

Her journey had been long. But Contessa's ultimate rise to prominence as National Security Advisor in 1998 assured that the rising political prodigy would be in the company of the world's most powerful people, something that greatly facilitated her exposure to the masses. But after a long, arduous campaign through the Midwest, where she debated Hillary Rodham Clinton in the largest televised Presidential debate in American History, she returned to Washington victorious, but feeling pummeled and drained. Even as President-Elect Brice was preparing to make the January 20th transition, emerging as the most powerful person on the planet, her personal physician wanted to introduce a mild sedative to help her untangle her nerves. Tess quickly declined, opting for a modified diet and new work-out regimen.

After a moment President Brice raised a hand, calling for quiet from the jubilant crowd.

As she stepped toward the polished podium, her brown business suit matching the soft sorrel of her cheeks, Tess felt a sense of pride and deference. This was indeed the First of many Firsts. Not only was Contessa Brice the first woman to hold the office of President, she was the first African American to do so as well. And to add fuel to the political fire, Contessa was a staunch Republican, overturning GOP convention while flipping the Democratic Party on its ear. The young political prodigy left her partisan Democratic opponents howling on the Hill, much like a pack of hungry coyotes, knowing that she was the only Republican they would never attempt to devour in the cauldron of public opinion. Contessa broke stereotypes like Sammy Sosa broke baseball bats. The minority voters, though generally inclined to vote Democratic, turned out in droves to vote for their Republican candidate.

The GOP fell in love with her right away, as well. A protégé of oil and Big Business, as well as color, femininity, and strength, the bright young executive was a shoe-in at the polls, and as she entered the second year of her term as President, Tess strove harder still to become the consummate executive and party loyalist. And the best way she knew how to do that was to illuminate the path of the great men who'd tread before her, to stand upon the shoulders of Presidents past and call their names, namely those history had shaded with controversy from what she termed the "Liberal Liability."

As the applause tailed off, President Brice cleared her throat and began; you could suddenly hear a pin drop:

"When my family told me that I could one day become President of the United States, I laughed. It was a good laugh, one that comes from conflicting emotions and years of doubt. It was a sensation mingled with fear and ambivalence. And when Martin Luther King recited his Dream Speech I never could have imagined that he was talking to me as well, that my dream could come true, and that I possessed some of the 'Content of Character' which has made this Nation the most powerful and proud."

She paused and her eyes began rolling across the many faces seated in the Press Box. "And I will see that this Nation continues to glean with pride."

Tess then launched into her ceremonial monologue.

"And the 37th President of the United States, Richard Milhouse Nixon, was one of the staunchest defenders of that freedom and pride. It was an unfortunate day when this political prodigy, having been the first American President to travel to China and Moscow, feverishly laying the groundwork for victory in Vietnam, will always be remembered for his failure in domestic politics. Indeed, President Nixon's untimely impeachment and abrupt exit from office stunned many while besmirching a stellar record of public service. Therefore, let us never forget the lessons that he taught before 1973."

Tess then turned, her eyes going to another section of the large crowd.

"Many of us seem to forget the failed attempts of prior administrations concerning our policy in Vietnam, something known as the Truman Doctrine, and the fact that Henry Kissinger, President Nixon's Secretary of State, received the Nobel Peace Prize, is, in itself, a call to remembrance."

Someone from CNN was standing near the press box.

"Oh, brother, she's playing the partisan card again."

The reporter next to him shrugged. "Who's going to stop her?"

"Despite her darkest days in the jungles of Vietnam, Laos and Cambodia," continued Contessa passionately. "We should always remember the headlines in the *Washington Post* for January 15th, 1973: 'End Of War In Vietnam! Hanoi Signs For Peace In Paris. American Troops To Return Home.'"

She then turned to the cenotaph itself, the enormous block of granite, the consummate headstone.

"The men who have ventured boldly before me have carried the torch of freedom through the darkest days, redefining both doctrine and constitution at every practical turn, a doctrine that eventually went on to include both black and white, red and brown, Indian and Asian, and Freedom's Bells will not be silenced. For it is in the very name of posterity itself that we are able to galvanize a resolve never before seen in the History of Mankind.

"Ladies and Gentlemen, we live and die in the greatest nation ever, a nation of ingenuity and faith, competitive markets and open worship, freedom of speech and the Bill of Rights! Ours is the truest of freedoms!"

A murmured hush swept through the audience.

"As Americans we realize that freedom comes with a price," continued the President, her tone hardening. "And sometimes that price can seem terribly high. But wherever we have stood, sometimes standing alone, we have always stood firm. We have never suffered defeat at home or abroad, from the Revolution of 1776 to the Second Korean War, and certainly including our valiant efforts and brilliant tactics in Vietnam."

President Brice drew a deep breath and continued.

"Whenever we have been called by Providence to exercise our enormous power and might in the pursuit of Freedom and Democracy, we have never faltered."

There was a tenuous and subdued roll of applause now, as if the crowd didn't understand many of her words, especially the younger members of the audience, who knew little, if anything, about some distant war in Vietnam.

But President Contessa Brice was going to call it exactly as she saw it. As she knew it.

# 10

The Oval Office had seated some of the greatest men in history, and as President Brice strolled behind her desk she could feel the essence of each, the trace residue of great power. She glanced at the Presidential Seal mounted to the wall behind her and smiled to herself. The polished redwood desk was neatly aligned with a stack of routine Intelligence reports from around the globe, as well as a lengthy letter from the Chairman of the Armed Forces Committee.

*Fitting enough,* thought Tess. *Considering it's Memorial Day.*

From the window the Jefferson Memorial could be seen shimmering in the distance, the marbled edifice nestled beyond the west lawn of the White House.

"I think you threw the crowd with that Vietnam eulogy," began Douglas Rollins, her White House chief of staff. Rollins had appeared before the room's conference table, fumbling with a stack of papers and a cell phone.

"I thought you were going to start talking about B-52s leveling Hanoi and Haiphong Harbor. You can relax now, Tess, the election is over."

President Brice chuckled lightly. She remembered why she'd chosen Douglas to lead her White House staff. Douglas didn't mince words. "I wasn't going to push the envelope, Doug, but someone had to at least place it on the table."

Her aide smiled. "You managed to do just that."

"Then my mission was accomplished," replied Tess smartly, smiling with her confident eyes. "After all, when was the last time the People heard the whole story of Vietnam, the fair and balanced edition? I mean, few Americans as it is know the difference between *Andrew* Jackson and *Stonewall* Jackson. We're going to address that problem in my next nationwide education proposal."

But Tess knew this was merely Doug's way of saying it wasn't such a good idea broaching the tender subject with such fervor. She knew her domestic aide well.

Contessa's mind suddenly went to something Douglas had said earlier. He was absolutely right about one thing: she was still feeling emotionally drained from the election. The Presidential crusade had the brass tacks of any partisan political battle, but got particularly nasty near the end, a sardonic slugfest that began drifting toward the *Springer*-esque. Senator Clinton had gone for the jugular, assigning a classical *Uncle Tom* label to the former NSA chief, one of her more desperate political maneuvers. But then Tess reached into a dirty bag of tricks, attacking the former attorney with disclosed information concerning some long-ago White Marsh dealings gone awry. Although the mud had flown in both directions, Contessa Brice went on to win that protracted battle, and was soon in position to voice her positions clearly and without fear of political reprisal. And she was prepared to do just that; her predecessor, George W., had taught her that from the very beginning.

But Hillary had stung her good, nevertheless, and Contessa frequently recalled the nationally televised debate which had fostered the political wildfire.

The televised "town meeting" between Hillary Rodham Clinton and Contessa Louise Brice drew record viewers and sent ratings through the roof. It was the first televised debate between two female Presidential candidates, two educated and brilliant women vying for the most powerful seat in government; and the world. Forget about the *Thrilla in Manila*, this duel was dubbed *Damsels In The District.*

And the battle was true to every pronunciation of hype.

"Dinner with Prime Minister Bertoldi is scheduled for seven," began Douglas evenly. "And we can meet for preliminary discussions around nine."

He again called her *Tess.*

Since Contessa was the first female President, the greeting of Ms., Mrs. or *Miss* President had not yet established a satisfying ring. Madam President was overly-formal, and Contessa preferred President Brice from members of the Press and Congressional leaders, and *Tess* from members of her Administration and White House staffers.

To Contessa, the personalized greeting was essential. And that's because Brice wore her administration like a suit of armor, another tactic she'd inherited from her predecessor.

For every *First* there was controversy, and this Presidency was certainly no exception. Tess wasn't taking any chances. She wanted a second term, since eight years in office would proffer an adequate window to incorporate her economic package as well as applying the finishing touches to the Nation's first missile defense system, something else her predecessor had passed along to her. And thus far, as her approval ratings soared, it was beginning to look as if she might even be able to get all of her economic strategies implemented.

"I've got that speech," rejoined Douglas, pulling her out of her pensive reverie. He presented her with a   type-written sheet of paper.

Tess took it but it wasn't actually a speech, rather a catalogue of ideas. Contessa Brice wrote her own speeches, another lesson she'd learned from the 43rd President. There would be no Sixteen-Word discrepancies, no sexing up charges, or sugar-coating solutions. Besides, if someone had tried to kill her father she would need only three words to fully express her intent, words to be exclaimed with plangent resolve, shouted from the White House lawn for the entire world to hear: *I Declare War!*

Contessa Brice was from the Old School of the *GOP*, with a grass-roots conservative philosophy certain to please both Big Business and the Military Establishment; it was a diplomatic agenda coupled with a Teddy Roosevelt, Rough Rider, boot-in-the-ass philosophy.

Indeed, Tess endeavored to appear dauntless in the world arena, stern and austere, especially in the wake of the Second Korean War; and she was ready to meet danger nose to nose on the battlefield if the moral circumstances dictated such. Her extension of America's anti-terror hegemony was an outright flexing of that muscle, something which not only challenged foreign adversaries, but threatened the entire liberal platform.

"We will not slip back into a shell of complacency and lethargy!" she'd cried during the televised debate. "We will stay vigilant as we lead this Crusade against Terror!"

And it was this very phraseology, brazen and defiant, that brought the hard-core leftists to the boiling point; but it was also that brash exterior which had won her the election.

After reviewing Doug's compendium of ideas, Tess went to the Truman Study, clutching the speech in one hand and hefting the Pentagon reports in the other. A fresh pot of tea was on the table near her desk, along with two porcelain mugs.

"The Israeli Prime Minister is comfortably tucked in, and has extended a heartfelt *Shalom, "* began Douglas, appearing at the table moments later. "He is eager to meet with you Tess. The formal Press briefing isn't scheduled until eleven o'clock tomorrow morning."

President Brice nodded.

Aaron Bertoldi was the was Young Turk of Israel, the Rising Star said to possess courage and wisdom, compassion and pragmatism. The Israeli centralists proclaimed that he inherited the wisdom of Solomon and the courage of David. Tess had met the young political prodigy only once before, and came away impressed with his candid and forthright intensity and guarded optimism. But she saw something else. Tess knew her instincts were honed well; and she saw uncertainty and an underlying sense of doubt. And she could feel the young charismatic leader turning to America for genuine guidance through the new and heightened sense of danger. President Brice could certainly understand why.

Douglas was leering at a newspaper, a scowl creeping across his face. "Walter Cronkite wrote another scathing article about the well-organized Right Wing Conspiracy. He's made the front page of the *New York Times* again this week. But it's got Hillary written all over it."

Tess fought off the urge to smile. Right Wing Conspiracy. Now that was a joke that had really lost its punch line. Here was a Republican-Female-African-American sitting in the White House; where were all these fat, balding white guys now? Huddled in the basement of the Pentagon? Or perhaps gathered in the upper reaches of the Capitol Building?

"Walter is a little behind the times," began Tess evenly. She was opening the file from the Senator of the Armed Forces Committee. "And to be honest, I really don't think he knows the difference between Alabama and the Alamo, despite his prehistoric and learned antiquity."

Douglas laughed, and studied his Commander-In-Chief with a sense of genuine affection. Tess was now the supreme executive and alpha diplomat, and she possessed a great sense of humor to go along with it. In this job, that was important. And despite her partisan platform and right wing agenda, Douglas saw flexibility and firm leadership within her, a dedicated sense of purpose, coupled with social compassion. Indeed, Contessa Brice was every bit the principled politician.

She deserved to win that election.

And she would serve the country well.

# 11
# Varanasi, India

The whistle sounded, blowing a sharp bleat across the jagged tree line.

For the many thousands of construction workers it was the sonorous sound of shift change, and the jungle trails began to swell with a deluge of trucks and pedestrian traffic.

And just as the second shift was returning from another day's work, the third was rolling from bed.

Their home became known as the *Green Village*. The sprawl of U.S. Army surplus tents lined the valley of *Borabi* at various intervals, sweeping along the hillsides of the Mondava Valley with stark efficiency. There were no hotels out here and many of the engineers, refusing to commute from Delhi every day, stayed in a cluster of trailers along Grid 10, while the skilled and unskilled laborers, mechanics and heavy equipment operators opted for the tents.

Tent Number 4 was more secluded than most, off the beaten path and alone in a gnarl of thickets. Mosquito screens lined the canvass windows and steel bunk beds were scattered loosely around. A large Zenith television sat in one corner, and kerosene lanterns were placed around the floor. None of the top bunks were occupied and the men used the available space for additional storage, or for playing checkers, chess and cards.

But tonight was poker night.

In the center of the room was a small clearing, replete with a stout wooden table and several folding chairs. The chairs were occupied, and five men were smoking cigarettes and swilling beer, preparing to gamble some, if not all, of their hefty bi-weekly paychecks. Piles of cash already littered the table, and empty beer cans abounded. Toni Cimino was the dealer, his fat fingers fanning the crisp cards like a swarm of locust. A Marlboro dangled from his lips, and one eye remained closed as a trail of cigarette smoke wafted across his tanned face. "Sixes are wild. Jacks or better to open."

There were grunts of acknowledgement and Toni began to deal, deftly flicking the cards to the various players.

Junior Jones was seated at one end of the table. The demolition expert was wearing a floppy fishing hat, and belched loudly before slowly fanning his hand.

"Hey, Black!" barked Junior. "Go grab another case of beer, will ya?"

Mark was laying quietly atop his bunk, a Stephen King novel cracked in the middle. He looked over the cover of *Salem's Lot*. "I ain't your waiter, Junior. Get the damn beer yourself."

"Can't you see I'm busy, Mark!" blared Junior, tossing a ten dollar bill into the pot. "Shit, man! What is your problemo, Amigo?"

Mark's eyes drifted back to the novel, but he could no longer concentrate, not that he could to begin with. He wished these ass-wipes would find another place to cut each other's throats. Ever since losing every penny of his earnings, Mark didn't want to hear the words poker, wild cards or antes. And now a roomful of jokers were shouting all three.

Bernie Klopper, a crane operator from Georgia, looked up. "What did you find up on 16, Mark? Some bones or something?"

"He found a *boner*, is more like it," cackled Junior. "He's hot for the Russian hoochie-mamma geologist."

Mark tried to ignore the comment, but winced inside.

*She's Ukrainian, you ass-wipe!* he thought to himself.

"Was it a mass grave, or something?" pressed Bernie, casually folding his hand.

Mark sighed. It was the fifth time that day he'd been asked to give a detailed report of the account. But before he could answer, Martin Zellar, Chief Supply Steward, hurried into the tent.

"Hey guys! Who wants to make a drive out to Grid 31?"

There were grunts of disapproval, and Junior reached for his beer. "Don't look at me," he said guardedly. "My day is done!"

"Me, neither," began Cimino, popping a fresh a can of Budweiser. "Besides, I've had too much to drink."

"Come on, fellas?" pressed Martin, a mock look of supplication. "Please don't make me pick one of you guys."

"What gives, anyway?" rejoined Cimino, drawing three cards for himself.

"Milton and some of the engineers are at the tunnel. They need some additional dual-cell batteries and another ohms-reader. Something's wrong with their gear."

No one replied and Martin continued to appraise the men.

"Don't everybody jump at once. How about you, Buddy?"

"Don't even think about it," replied the swarthy truck mechanic from Eros and Son's. "I've got fifteen hours overtime already this week."

"Why not go for an even twenty?" chortled Martin, drawing closer to the table.

"Nope," said Reynolds firmly. "I'm gonna get my overtime right here at this table."

Martin turned toward Mark, who was laying quietly on his bunk.

"How about you, Black? Feel like taking a little ride?"

"It's not a little ride," replied Mark tiredly.

Martin shrugged, then lit a cigarette. He slowly approached the table, his search for a volunteer temporarily forgotten. "Whose got the bank?"

Eyes drifted to Dennis O'Reilly, a rig operator for Central Pacific. The Irish national had a jumbled pile of Tens and Twenties stacked before him. Everyone had piles of crumpled bills atop the table, as well as a splay of coins, but O'Reilly unquestionably held the bank.

"Talk to O'Reilly," wheezed Junior. "He's got a four leaf clover up his ass tonight."

The truck driver smiled, tugging down on the rim of his Yankees baseball cap. "Luck of the Irish, I would imagine."

No one saw Junior's hand reach inside his boot.

"I'll go," croaked Mark, dropping his book atop the bunk and standing. "These assholes won't let me sleep anyway. What am I driving?"

"Take the Chevy outside," began Martin, tossing him a fat key chain. "And bring it right back, Black. I'll need it to get over to supply in the morning."

"10-4," acknowledged Mark, grabbing his flannel shirt and starting for the door.

"Don't get lost, Don Juan!" barked Junior from his seat. "The last thing we want to do is pull your ass out of a mud pit somewhere!"

"Fuck off, Junior!" replied Mark, slamming the screen door behind him.

"Don't get mad at me!" blathered Junior. "I didn't tell you to stand on a pair of Queens!"

As the room erupted into a thunderous roll of laughter, Mark mashed the accelerator and sped off into the night.

He could feel the confrontation coming. It was all a matter of time.

*And he'd probably been stacking the deck the whole time!* thought Mark angrily. *Either that, or he's got Seattle Slew's horse shoe up his ass. The dickhead is simply too lucky! And he has a real big mouth!*

"When I get back I'll straighten him out," hissed Mark, slowing now and creeping along the dark trail. He could hear the engineers communicating over the radio and it sounded like they were in complete disagreement over ongoing procedures. Something about right-degree angles and structural integrity. Occasionally, he would hear the voice of Milton Hickers crackling aloud, regulating the dispute like a referee in a prize fight. The old man would make the final decision, but he let his people hammer it out, getting the full story from all sides at the same time. Before making a final judgment, Hickers put an argument on trial.

As Mark listened to the chatter, his eyes rolled through the pitch black surroundings. Junior was right about one thing: it *was* dark back here. Only occasionally did the moon creep through the clouds, for which he was grateful. The forty mile trek was exacerbated by the condition of the road, which wasn't exactly a road at all.

Well, certainly not by American standards.

# 12
# Grid 31

The drive took nearly two hours, and Mark knew he was getting close when he saw the luminescent glow of Halogen spotlights washing through the trees ahead. Grid 31 was lit up as if it were two o'clock in the afternoon rather than two in the morning. Heavy equipment and light trucks were parked everywhere, and long portable tables held urns of coffee, boxes of crullers, and tubes of blueprints. And just ahead was the enormous tunnel, its mouth carved out of a wall of granite.

A noisy Razorback suddenly swept out of the enormous portal, its bristling porcupine spinning at several thousand revolutions a minute. Mark made sure the enormous piece of heavy equipment was well clear before driving slowly into the yawning shaft, strings of lights leading the way. He felt like Jonah entering the mouth of the great fish.

Mark noticed that the topside catwalks had already been installed, and he spotted a group of men standing deep inside the shaft. As Mark drove into the mountain he turned his headlights to hi-beam, and the smell of sulfur and dampness began filling his nostrils.

The architects and engineers were standing near an electrical control panel, about one-hundred yards inside the entrance. As it turned out, something was wrong with their ohm-readers.

All six of them.

As Mark approached his headlights flashed across the scowl of Milton Hickers; Mark pulled gently to a stop.

After unloading several boxes of supplies, he looked around the giant bunker. The tunnel was undoubtedly the cornerstone of the entire operation. It was designed to accommodate twin locomotives and looked more like an

65

aircraft hangar than a train tunnel. In a matter of several short years freight lines and giant diesel locomotives would be rolling through here, the big MR 105s, each one-hundred feet long and packed with turbine. Two of the powerhouses could pass one another in here, roaring only inches abreast, chains of box cars and oil tankers in tow.

And despite all of his recent misfortune, Mark felt an rare pang of pride.

After only several moments of listening to their heated discussion, it became clear what was troubling the structural engineers. They were beginning to encounter a network of caverns and caves throughout the walls of the manmade tunnel. As Mark accompanied the group deeper into the shaft, he learned that the caves were the result of moisture erosion, perhaps the result of natural springs. But one architect insisted that the caves had been dug recently, and that they were the result of technological planning.

"All of them at right angles, with a forty-five-degree pitch," insisted the architect. "Complete uniformity, and identical in size!"

His thesis carried little weight with the others. No one at Pendleton & Waxler could have dug them, and without dynamite or Razorbacks, they ruled out the possibility of a man-made excavation. At one point during the debate, Hickers turned to Mark and forced a smile:

"Mr. Black, would you do me a tremendous favor and bring in one of the hydraulic lifts from outside?"

"The keys should be in the ignition," broke in a structural engineer. "We need to take a look at something."

"Yes, sir," snapped Mark, feeling privileged to be in the company of the corporate Big Wigs. He left the tunnel and went to a 2.5 ton GMC truck with an attached bucket and lift. The keys were indeed in the ignition, and Mark rumbled back into the tunnel moments later, the truck's diesel roar reverberating loudly in the cavernous portal.

He parked the truck alongside the men, directly beneath one of the unusual caverns they'd discovered. Additional lights were pointed at the dark hole near the ceiling, and everyone was craning their necks.

Knowing fully how to operate the machine, Mark volunteered his services and he, Milton Hickers and another man went up, the bucket rising like an elevator. Mark fingered the levers, and drew them closer to the black hole, their shadows slanting across the rock wall.

"What is that smell?" gasped Milton, waving his hand across his face. "It smells like an open grave, for Christ's sake!"

Everyone was in agreement, and when they leveled off Milton pointed a flashlight into the mysterious cavity. The oval walls were jagged, a spiraling mosaic of pointed nooks of cut rock. They immediately ruled out water as an erosion catalyst. As far as depth, the beam of light was immediately swallowed up in the deepest recesses of the shaft.

"Looks like it runs quite a ways," groaned Milton. "Who wants to climb in there and have a look around?"

Both men leered at Mark.

After slipping off his shirt, Mark stood on the railing of the lift, most of his weight on one foot, and reached for the wall.

"Watch your step!" spluttered Hickers, boosting him up from the backside. "And hold your breath! It might be a vent straight from hell!"

Mark groaned, placing the tip of his boot in a small crevice. With a push of his arms, and a slight lunge, he stepped inside the cave's mouth. He had just enough room to stand fully erect, and could feel warm air blowing across him, the source unknown.

"It leads outside, I think," began Mark, squinting into the darkness. It was also warm and clammy, like a submarine's boiler room. "I can tell by the press of air."

Mark stepped further down the corridor, his flashlight beam dancing down the black funnel and into oblivion. He then pointed the beam to the ground and discovered the source of the unpleasant smell. There were what appeared to be animal droppings in the cave, tall mounds of black, tarry feces.

He noticed three piles of the shiny dung.

"Looks like something took a healthy dump up here, Mr. Hickers!" croaked Mark. "And more than once!"

"Animal shit?" boomed Milton's voice, echoing down the cave.

Mark picked up a crooked branch and began prodding at the substance. "That's an affirmative, sir."

"Can you get me a sample?" asked Hickers, his voice echoing crassly.

Mark turned back, a spurned look on his face. "Just what am I supposed to carry it in?"

Milton produced a white handkerchief, and balled it up in his fist. "A gift from my late wife. I never use that damn thing, anyway!"

Using the stick, Mark shuffled a gooey scoop of dung into the white cloth, before partially folding it up.

He returned to the bucket and hurled the stick toward the ground, clear of the men below. He then handed the specimen to Hickers, who promptly passed it to the engineer.

"A fine job, young man," began Hickers, helping Mark back into the bucket. "A fine, fine job."

When they rejoined the others, the debate began raging again. Mark stood quietly off to the side, a neutral observer. But they soon turned on him, firing a staccato of questions. Mark said that he didn't see any signs of stalagmite or stalactite, signs of antiquity, and he explained the warm gush of air. But rather than solve anything, it sent the voices rising again.

"I didn't see any signs of water or water erosion, either," he added. "It seems like a fresh dig, but I'm not an expert."

"And animal shit doesn't change a thing!" grumbled Arthur Hamilton, a torsion specialist from Kroeger & *Rogers*. "You could find a T-Rex in there, and it wouldn't change a thing!"

That was certainly true, especially considering the historic and nostalgic ineptitude of Milton Hickers. But Milton seemed to take the sarcasm as a personal affront.

"I just want to know what the hell we're dealing with!" roared Hickers, his jowls jiggling with rage. "If something is climbing into my railroad tunnel, I want to know about it! And if it just happens to be *human* feces," he continued, holding up the shit-filled handkerchief. "We've got a whole new set of circumstances at hand!"

Mark agreed, and was every bit as curious as Milton.

Mark then glanced behind him. He noticed one of the architects gazing at the stony floor. The man then leaned over and picked up the stick discarded earlier by Mark. But as it turned out, it wasn't a stick at all. Under the lights now, it looked like a giant piece of insect antennae.

"Did you find this up there?" asked the electrician, slipping on his reading glasses and peering intently at the feeler.

"Yea," replied Mark. "I thought it was a stick, and tossed it down."

"Have a look at this, Milton," said the man, moving toward Hickers. "Just what in the hell do you make of that?"

Milton touched the unusual cynosure. "Looks like it belongs on a horseshoe crab."

"I don't think we have a crustacean problem, Mr. Hickers." someone chided.

Someone else joined in on the light ribbing: "It's Voltair/Buffon all over again!"

Milton wasn't amused.

"That's it! It's settled!" barked Hickers, raising his arms in frustration.

"We're going ahead with the tunnel! At least until something becomes an imminent and undeniable threat! A few small caverns shouldn't pose much of a risk. Seal up those cave entrances so we don't have some crazy animals falling onto moving trains, and get this hole dug!"

It was settled, and everyone began departing, like lawyers following a jury's verdict. Mark followed them out, still wondering what kind of animal wandered twenty-five miles into the side of a mountain.

"Hey, Mr. Black!" rang out the voice of Milton Hickers. Mark turned to the freight magnate.

"When you get back to camp notify the men that we're back on line tomorrow morning. Pendleton & Waxler will be staying on with the dig here."

*Don't do us any favors,* thought Mark, forcing a smile.

"Yes, sir, Mr. Hickers."

# 13

After Mark made the long drive back to the *Green Village* it was nearing seven a.m. The sun was slowly burning off a haze of jungle moisture, and as Mark approached the camp's fuel depot an impulse began pulling at him. He suddenly decided not to go straight back to his tent, and instead wheeled across a grassy field.

He would take a chance on locating Tatiana's trailer.

The sexy anthropologist had said it was parked somewhere off Grid 16, and that it might be a little *"defecuwt to fine."* But Mark didn't mind looking, and he didn't have to look long. After rolling over a steep bank of dead vines, he spotted the Ranchero sticking out of the trees near the Delhi Road, its canopy opened. Although he'd come uninvited, Mark didn't think Tatiana would mind. The look in her eyes that night on *Grid 16* told him she wouldn't; and he'd read her correctly.

Tatiana greeted Mark at the door with a warm smile and bright eyes. She came out into the sunlight, drawing close and extending a hand. The attractive anthropologist was brimming as she recited the latest weather report, and slowly they walked toward a glade over the hill.

Tatiana turned toward the enormous horn of Everest, using her hand to shield the sun from her eyes.

"They had to think it reached into the Heavens," she said pensively. "In fact, it is India's very own 'Stairway to Heaven.'"

Mark smiled. He knew it wasn't a stairway to heaven. It was the result of tectonic plates, the shifting of the Earth's crust, the outpouring of magma and molten nickel. And despite her aesthetic disposition, Mark knew Tatiana fully understood the amazing birthing processes of these life sustaining wonders. It was cosmos verses chaos, Yin and Yang, good and evil.

After a moment of reflection Tatiana invited Mark into her trailer, and the heavy equipment operator cantered inside the Ranchero, not exactly sure what to expect. Her office was dim, and his eyes swept around like a sightseer in an antique shop. A metal desk was covered with bottles and cruets of different chemicals. He could also make out a *Bunsen* burner and propane torch, as well as a rack of various vials, each marked with tiny labels. He remembered the chemistry kit he'd gotten back in high school.

"Looks cozy," said Mark, turning toward Tatiana. The scholar looked fresh and vibrant, her eyes keen and sharp, her lips pursed with contentment. The Ukrainian woman appeared comfortable as well, donning loose Khaki shorts and a blue blouse, with the tails tied in front. Mark detected the sweet scent of jasmine. It was his favorite. Just how she managed to stay so fresh and inviting out here in the brush would remain a mystery to him.

Mark readily accepted her hospitality and joined Tatiana for a light breakfast, pulling up a seat near her desk and nibbling on some fruit, rye bread, and a jar of strawberry preserves she kept stashed in her bag. Tatiana apologized for the lack of modern amenities, and Mark only chuckled.

"What exactly do you do in your profession?" he finally asked, spreading some preserves across a heal of bread.

Tatiana nodded and drew a noticeable breath.

"I look for answers."

"What are the questions?"

"Anthropological Anatomization is much like Archaeological Identification. Chronology is based solely on two separate and principled theories. *Contemporaneity* and *Sequence*. And the first thing we look for is *stratigraphy.*"

Mark nodded, as if he actually understood her explanation. But he wasn't at all listening to Tatiana's brilliant description of her work. He was watching the purse of her full Slavic lips, and the soft blue sparkle of her eyes, now wide with excitement and passion.

As Mark listened he knew he was in the presence of a woman who genuinely loved her profession. Here was a person who was living out their life's passion, and he felt oddly inspired by her Promethean approach to life. Mark then began to realize that he didn't know too many people who danced to the beat of their own drum, who broke stride with the rank and file and went off into the jungles of life. Alone. That's because everyone was hooked with the Nine-To-Five Syndrome. Get the house, and you've lived out your patriarchal responsibility. Get the car and you'll find the girl, that leads to the family, and then you start running out the clock, waiting to put in your twenty years of obedient service to get the pension you need to survive.

Yea, everyone he knew had the world by the balls, all right. And as we all steadily conformed to the "system," as we begrudgingly turned the wheels of progress, we gradually surrendered our inner passions and dreams to the truly wealthy. The final phase of the lonely saga is to simply fade into unmentionable mediocrity and fiscal obscurity.

But that wasn't the case with Tatiana.

"Your Bohemian lifestyle suites you well," began Mark, when she finally paused. "I envy what you have."

"Thank you, Mark," twittered the attractive scholar, as if she'd already read his every thought. She smiled, and began to percolate. "Let me get something."

Tatiana went to her desk and withdrew a large magnum of champagne, before plucking two mason jars off the chemistry shelf. "This was to be saved for the special occasion, when my team and I discovered the next great mystery," she began cheerily. "But my team never materialized beyond Ahmel, and so far we haven't quite reached the Promised Land."

She then paused, her eyes fluttering. "But I think I may have already discovered what I have been searching for."

Mark had no idea what that was supposed to mean. Was she talking about him? Or the bones she fond on Grid 15, the contorted thorax and enormous skull? He surely hoped it was the former.

Mark studied the sultry roll of her hips as she turned and approached him, then easing herself onto a throw pillow on the floor. "They are not the best glasses," she said handing him a mason jar. "But it is not the best vintage."

She then passed the hefty bottle to Mark. "Would you do the honors?"

With a loud plonk the cork shot across the room, and golden froth began spilling across Mark's fingers.

"What exactly are you looking for out here?" began the dozer operator, pouring two jars of wine.

"The basis of my theses," replied Tatiana, not bothering to elucidate.

"You mean, like, for a book?"

"Not a book," she chirped. "A dissertation."

Tatiana explained that she was preparing to receive her doctorate's degree in anthropology. At this stage of her journey she needed only to successfully defend her scientific dissertation, an archaeological compendium delineating the Hittite migration, and eventual assimilation, into the Indus Valley.

In between sips from her mason jar, she began telling Mark about her life's passion, about her interest in Mesopotamia, Egypt, and the evolution of certain cultures.

"I like to study the ebb and flow of civilization," she continued firmly. "The shifting tides of power, from Mesopotamia, to Egypt, then Greece to Rome, and finally Britain and America. What I see is a fascinating reflection of multi-cultural cross-pollination."

Tatiana spoke as if defending the controversial dissertation that very moment, and seemed very much on the ball now.

"Many of us are aware of the ancient pyramids, the Sphinx, and hieroglyphics," continued the scholar. "But there are many sub-civilizations which have branched off and persisted. The Dorian Sea Peoples, the Hittites, Arminius and the Germans. There are literally thousands. And although many of these cultures are not studied or documented at great length, they are equally important concerning Civilization's impact and scope."

Mark was impressed; but before he could extend a compliment, a sound crackled from the back room. The static hiss was repeated, and someone's voice began crackling over a radio. Mark was startled. He even recognized the voice of Harry Belcher, fuel delivery driver. Mark looked to Tatiana, his eyes asking for an explanation.

Again the scanner crackled to life, and he heard Harry Belcher saying: "Got to make a run to 31, and then I'm on the way, over."

"10-4," replied a heavy equipment operator. "You'd better hurry. I see a crew coming along with extra rebar now, over."

Tatiana smiled self-consciously. "Forgive the interruption. It is a radio scanner. I occasionally monitor the radio traffic. It is the only way I am able to get to a site so quickly."

"Pretty inventive," said Mark.

And it was.

*And that helps explain how you were on* 16 *so quickly that night.*

"Would you like to see some of my work?" asked Tatiana, eager to change the subject.

"Why not?" replied Mark, wondering what other surprises she had up her sleeve. He was feeling the first tingles of a warm buzz.

Tatiana returned to her desk and pulled a bundle of newspapers from the bottom drawer.

She gently unwrapped the jumble and approached Mark. She seemed to be holding a flat rock. But as she approached he saw it was a clay tablet.

"This is a bas-relief," began the young woman purposefully. "And it dates back to the 16th Century, A.D. It was written by a Brahmin, and tells of a strange light descending from the sky and landing on, or near, the Himalayan Valley."

Tatiana laid the stone on the floor between them, and hefted a large text from the bookshelf. After flipping through the pages for a moment, she opened the book and handed it to Mark.

"You are looking at something much older, written in Aramaic by an ancient Hittite sect, presumably a high priest of the order. Only the Hittite priests possessed the literacy level to interpret astronomy and record law."

Mark studied the picture. "What's the connection?"

"They mention the same eerie light descending toward the valley. The exact same lore from distant and unassociated Peoples."

The tablets certainly looked like they belonged under glass in a museum, but they did little to ignite a flux of curiosity. Besides, Mark thought it was a pretty weak connection.

"Last summer," continued Tatiana, crossing her arms. "I took this bas-relief to a renowned archaeologist in Frankfurt, a professor of stratigraphy at the Institute Of Fossilization. He was able to translate the markings. And its part of the reason why I am here. Another part of the puzzle."

Mark was gazing at the tablet now.

"What does it say?"

"It tells of a ritualistic sacrifice to a deity, as conducted by the Aryans."

As if by magic, Tatiana then produced a small ebony carving. The trinket was about eight inches long, and Mark thought it looked like something from Greek or Roman mythology, something he'd once seen in a *Sinbad* movie.

"This rare artifact has been damaged by the elements, but it is an alleged replication of that deity."

"Of what?"

"Of what the Hittites called *Kretta*," she said in an eerie calm. "It means *Ground Dweller*."

The statue was interesting, but it didn't prove a thing. If her dissertation was based on these artifacts, Mark estimated that she had a lot of research remaining ahead.

"*Vedic* scripture mentions them several times as well, and a papyrus found in Byzantium states a startlingly similar description."

She then flipped to a page showing two cuneiform basalt tablets, written in Aramaic by the Hittites. "The Hittites possessed, at one time, a highly advanced form of society, with their own high priests, gods, and forms of worship. I think they were sacrificing to something they thought was a god.

I saw the temples throughout the valley. The Sumerian term for offering is *entok.* It is mentioned frequently. *"*

Mark tried to look interested as Tatiana motioned to the book.

"These were discovered in *Ur,* the city in southern Iraq. It is the birthplace of the patriarch Abraham."

Hungry. He was getting hungry. Mark watched her mouth moving, but thought about a double-cheeseburger with fries and an ice cold *Coke.*

"In my profession," continued the ravenous scholar. "One must first learn to read and interpret a vast array of clues. And as I mentioned earlier, it is very important to learn the language of stratification."

More than satisfied with her lengthy reply, Mark nodded in agreement and his eyes roamed casually around the trailer. It was also clear from first glance that Tatiana was a bibliophile of sorts, and he began scanning some of the titles scattered across the shelves. *"'Egypt Beyond The Cataracts, '"* he said evenly. *"'Mesopotamia: Land of Eden?'"* and *"'Darwin Explained.'"*

Then he tried, unsuccessfully, to pronounce another title.

*"Koea..., Koalehcan..."*

*"'Selacanth,'"* replied Tatiana instantly (but spelled *Coelacanth*). "It is a prehistoric fish thought to be extinct for fifty million years."

"Thought to be?" replied Mark, pulling down the book.

Tatiana nodded. "They found one in 1938. Off the coast of South Africa. It was quite a surprise, a fish with fins for swimming, and appendages to begin the process of walking. A genuine paradox, possessing both gills and lungs. A clear link in the chain."

Mark sighed, and stretched out on the floor. "So, what ever got you interested in bones? I mean, it's not what people normally set out to do. I've never even met an archaeologist before now."

Tatiana perked up, eager to reply.

"To begin with, I am not an archaeologist, as you keep saying. I am an anthropologist, and it is my job to study anthropoids, or apes, from which we are thought to have evolved."

Mark arced his brow, trying to look a little naive.

"Don't you believe in the Bible's Creation explanation? The story of Adam and Eve?"

Tatiana smiled. "I do. And since the Bible speaks metaphorically, Creationism is often misinterpreted."

He knew he would regret it, but he asked anyway:

"What do you mean?"

Tatiana drew a deep breath. "When our first simian ancestors climbed out of the trees, electing to live their lives on the ground, a process dictated by their evolving mental facilities and intellect, then freedom of choice and independent thought was born. This is represented as the Tree Of Knowledge."

That was a mouthful and Mark wondered if she was finished.

She wasn't.

"Nature takes care of its own. Instinct, evolutionary adaptation, and pheromones dictate to the animal world. All animals are guided by these innate navigational systems, since their rational intellect is rather useless.

"But once we climbed from the trees, down from this Garden Of Eden where Nature dictated our actions, we separated ourselves. We were no longer subject to Nature's rule."

Mark started to speak, but Tatiana continued: "It is now the human intellect that guides human action. Not innate orders from Nature. By making our own choices, we have sinned against Nature."

"That's pretty incredible," replied Mark with a ring of sincerity. "I have never heard it put so beautifully."

"Like *Noah's Ark*," she continued, slowly swirling the jar of wine. "The parable of the Great Flood is another good example."

Mark was looking confused now. He was expecting another mysterious and enigmatic explanation. Tatiana didn't disappoint him.

"The story of the Great Flood may be God's way of explaining the passing of the dinosaurs and the birth of a New Era. Perhaps He became displeased with the great reptiles, and they were not permitted on the Ark of Evolution. As the Biblical serpent has been barred from the Garden Of Eden, so too have dinosaurs been barred from Earth. Can you see that message cloaked in there? Rather than explaining the size and shape of the meteor he hurled down, he explained the emergence of the mammal."

As Mark listened, Tatiana began studying him harder.

*He is definitely All-American*, she thought with a sense of arousal. Mark reminded her of a character out of an old American western she'd once read many nights ago. And that made her feel a tickle of excitement. Tatiana had always been fascinated with America and its immense prosperity, but it was her People which intrigued her the most. And this one seemed to epitomize the average American man, rugged and interesting in his own tall, strong and handsome way.

She burned with curiosity, wondering what this Yankee was like, this rugged Aryan with the noticeably Anglican bloodline. His look and temperament, as well as his height and build, had immediately appealed to her. Yes, she liked the study of anthropology, and at that very moment none more intrigued her than the American construction worker.

*And he has a nice pushka,* she thought coyly.

The unusual circumstances made her think of a Tarzan and Jane movie she had seen as a child, and Tatiana nearly chuckled, feeling a nostalgic pang of pleasure.

Mark was lifting a large textbook off the shelf. "So, are we ever going to find the Lost City of Atlantis?"

Tatiana smiled, pushing the American's cute *pushka* from her mind.

"The Lost City of Atlantis is a prophecy," she began assuredly. "Not an actual place."

Mark arced an eyebrow. "I've never heard that before."

Tatiana shrugged, and began wrapping the loaf of rye.

"Like so many of the biblical lessons, this one may also be taken out of context."

Mark leaned back and crossed his arms, giving her the floor. Tatiana gladly took it. "Atlantis is a state of social perfection that will never be, rather than a particular place," she began evenly, rearranging the objects scattered across her desk. "Some say Atlantis currently refers to the Way of the West, where a zenith of socio-political-economic harmony has been best attained."

"I think I like that explanation," said Mark, replacing the book and grabbing another.

"But there are always elements that wish to destroy that structure," continued Tatiana, as if reciting a   well-rehearsed script. "…a structure that may be represented as a remaining stronghold. Every vanguard civilization has had to endure the Atlantis phenomenon: Mesopotamia, Athens, Rome, Tokyo. And now it is the West and its ways. These forces will eternally threaten the proverbial city of Atlantis, which is never quite lost, but which may some day succumb to the barbarian masses, much as Rome met its end."

"Like with Attila the Hun?" offered Mark. "Or Genghis Khan?"

Tatiana nodded. "Sometimes. But other times it may manifest itself in the form of a Fifth Column, a national mutiny, the catalysts of destruction emerging from within. New people, with different religious preferences, language, moral platforms and global outlooks will stand at the ready. Already firmly entrenched in the streets, the hamlets and villages become transformed quickly."

Tatiana suddenly looked as if her own words were frightening her. "It was like that with the communists, when the Red December came to town. Even our Christmas changed."

Tatiana suddenly fell silent, as if she'd said too much already. Something about the American began making her nervous, and she was beginning to feel a little vulnerable.

"Forgive my theoretical tangent," she began, standing and walking slowly away from her desk.

Mark stood as well, and went to her. They were only inches apart now, gazing silently into the smoldering eyes of one another.

Tatiana's gaze almost seeming to say: *"What are you waiting for? I'm a woman, you're a man, and we're both out here in the middle of the jungle!*

Mark felt poised to respond.

*So, she wants a sexual tryst right out here in the Ranchero?* he thought excitedly, a lascivious vision prancing across his mind. *That would be just dandy, too!*

Although a little surprised by her timing, Mark almost felt obligated to respond, feeling a pleasurable urge working up his loins, like a puma dancing nimbly up a tree.

But as he was about to spring, the trailer door swung open and Ahmel stumbled in, breathing heavily and looking exhausted. He was still carrying his rifle, and looked as if he'd been running through the jungle all night.

"I have given them the specimens," he spluttered in broken English. "They said it can take up to a month for the results to come back here. He said we must be patient."

"Thank you, Ahmel," replied Tatiana, her tone surprisingly stoic. "You have been a tremendous help. It is a pleasure working with you, My Friend. I hope you decide to extend your assignment, as I would love to keep you on beyond the semester."

Now it was Ahmel who was smiling. "It would certainly look good for my resume, Ms. Borosky. Are we going out into the field again tomorrow?"

"Bright and early, Ahmel!" chimed the anthropologist. "We must see what else the earth reveals!"

In a way, Mark was grateful for the interruption. So much was answered in so few words. As he'd initially feared, Ahmel was not her lover. He was her employee, her friend at best. This was strictly a scholastic relationship, and following this encounter Mark felt certain there was nothing more to it.

After delivering the news, Ahmel departed, closing the door gently behind him.

"Just where does he stay?" asked Mark.

Tatiana was gazing at the door. "Oh, he has his places."

Tatiana then began moving away, and Mark felt a pang of regret when she glanced at her thick leather watchband.

"I have a few things to do before nightfall," she began softly. "But, if you like, you can come past later tonight and I could really show you something of interest."

Mark smiled, and stepped slowly toward her. His lips swept her cheek.

"I would love to," he whispered, his voice low and brusque. "I'll bring a little dinner or something. You must be getting hungry."

Tatiana had a mischievous look in her eye. "That would be very nice."

# 14

But for Mark, it would not be a clean getaway.

As he stood and went to the door of the Ranchero, he remembered why he'd come here in the first place, and his eyes were sharp with recognition.

"I almost forgot," began Mark matter-of-factly. "There's actually another reason I came by today. I was up on Grid 51 early this morning. Something really weird is going on up there."

Tatiana's eyes revealed her total captivation, and she seemed to stop breathing. Like a cat stalking through the bush, she leaned forward in silence, her blue eyes boring into his.

"What are you talking about, Mark?" she said softly. "Could you be a little more specific?"

"There are caves in our cave," he said in a whisper, leaning now toward her now.

But there would be no passionate hug and romantic kiss. Tatiana tore away her eyes and stood, before pacing the floor anxiously. "What do you mean, Mark? How could you forget this? This may be of great importance to my research!"

Mark settled back atop the desk. "Well, it appears that something, some animals, may have been borrowing through the mountain. It's the weirdest thing the engineers have ever seen. Milton Hickers was even there. He runs the railroad, and nobody knows what to think."

Tatiana lurched toward him, her eyes wide with excitement. "Can you get me in there?"

Mark shrugged. "I may be able to…"

"And let me get me some pictures, if you can!" spluttered Tatiana, continuing her nervous pacing.

"You don't know the half of it," offered Mark. "We found some kind of animal droppings. Black and real smelly."

Tatiana froze. You would have thought he'd just announced a cure for cancer. Her hand went to her breast, as if to slow the beat of her heart. After a moment, she drew a deep breath, sighing.

"Mark Black, we need to have a little talk."

It bordered on the bizarre. And as Mark listened to the incredible story, as he studied her eyes gazing up, as if expecting to see the perfect words floating across the ether, he felt a growing chord of skepticism. Prolonged exposure to the jungle could affect the mind after a while, any isolated place could, and people reacted differently to new and unfamiliar surroundings. Was it possible that this Ukrainian beauty had tinkered slightly off her emotional square, possibly dropping a few marbles in her drive for educational and professional excellence?

*Stranger things have happened.*

Or perhaps it was the effects of the booze.

*Alien creatures.*

*Hittite gods.*

*Wow.*

"And the artifacts you provided are a big piece of the story!" she stammered excitedly.

Mark gazed into her eyes and nodded. "I'm glad I could help."

But even as he said this, Mark detected some red flags of concern, and he began wondering how he could somehow help her through this troubling state of mind. He even began to feel a pang of pity mixed in there somewhere, and he hoped he was wrong. Perhaps she was indeed on the brink of a fascinating discovery; but until that fully developed, he decided he should try to keep an eye on her.

Mark stood and glanced at his watch. He couldn't believe he'd been there three hours already.

"My shift will be starting in about an hour," said Mark, grabbing his flannel and moving to the door. "Like I said, I'll bring you back something later. Something to eat. A sandwich, or some soup. You probably haven't been eating too well out here. It's really important to get all your vitamins and stuff."

Tatiana smiled. "That would be very nice. And then maybe I can actually show you what I have discovered."

Feeling a sense of settled resolve, Mark went to Tatiana and kissed her cheek. He could tell she'd been expecting a kiss on the lips. Her head had rolled ever so slightly toward him.

That could wait.

# 15
# The White House
# Washington D.C.

When Douglas Rollins wasn't with the President, or the Press, or the Pentagon People, he was coordinating the President's schedule, sometimes down to the last second. And although Contessa Brice often devised her own itinerary, he remained nearby nevertheless, revamping his efforts to accommodate the needs and desires of his Boss. It was a 24-hour a day profession, something that did not surprise the former mathematician.

But when the U.S. Congress finally announced their annual break, not scheduling to reconvene until mid-June, Doug's duties began tailing off. And when President Brice decided to vacation at Camp David in the hills of Maryland, the White House became as quiet as a monastery.

For the first time in a very long time the White House chief of staff looked forward to some peace and quietude.

The first day of this brief sabbatical was liberating, and Douglas would only spend a few minutes at the White House today. He needed only to check the status of the tenement's various in-house personnel, before catching a short flight to New Jersey where he was scheduled to speak at his *alma mater*.

Visiting the vaunted halls which had so deeply impacted his political career remained important to Douglas Rollins. It was good karma to remember where you came from, and the halls of Princeton, with its vaulted ceilings and laureate heritage, always reflected a calm, soothing confidence. It was here that Douglas formed his political views and moral foundations, a burgeoning which eventually led him to Washington and catapulted him into his current occupation.

But mathematics were his true calling, his gift, and Douglas merely accepted the offer from Washington out of diplomatic etiquette rather than personal desire. He'd known Tess in the early days, when they were classmates, when Doug wore his hair like Jim Morrison, and Tess was a fiery member of the debating committee. And although he would serve the President well, Douglas's thoughts were always with numbers, that universal language of science.

The college lecture hall was packed cedar panel to cedar panel with students, and Dean Whittaker was in attendance, seated in the rear of the assembly hall and trying unsuccessfully to look anonymous.

A speaker from Cal Tech was there, as well. The radiological physicist was scheduled to address the student body following Douglas. He seemed oblivious to the roomful of students and continued reviewing a campus pamphlet as he awaited his turn at the lectern.

Douglas recalled the series of events which changed his life. He had initially dreamed of working for NASA. What a difference a semester could make. Within a matter of eight weeks, his life's direction took a completely unexpected turn, a political One-Eighty.

"The *Orno* Factor," began Douglas, standing at a podium now. "It is the product of what we term *evolutionary mathematics*, something that feeds itself, as well as the scientist."

Douglas felt a sliver of excitement twirling up his spine. Numerical equations were his passion, and it was here that Doug's mind raced across equations like a cheetah across the Serengeti.

"And when Ali Jabbar devised the mathematical language which became known as *Algebra,* we were again looking at the magic of *Orno*! For it is these stepping stones that each generation provides which enables the next to further the goal, the goal of understanding the laws of Nature, and to one day control these laws as we have already begun!

"And as long as we strive for morality, our goals as well as our end should be clear from the beginning," continued Douglas passionately. "And that is to better the human condition. Your efforts are beyond righteous. They are noble."

Douglas went on to praise the work of Einstein, Newton, and Galileo, before rolling into another monologue.

"And upon the shoulders of those who have gone before us, we will stare into the future!"

After acknowledging the efforts of the Princeton Sciences Department, and speaking at length about NASA's ongoing space programs, Douglas asked for questions.

But the works of Newton and Einstein were the last things these kids wanted to discuss.

"What are your responsibilities to the President?"

"Do you see her every day?"

"What is she like?"

The language of physics disappeared.

"Does she try to emulate Margaret Thatcher?" asked one student. "She seems like she might become known as the *Iron Butterfly*. Can you explain that general sentiment?"

Douglas looked to the ceiling for a moment. Then his eyes were drawn down. "I think the President's inner strength is the result of one salient attribute."

Douglas paused, and looked slowly around the room. There was total silence. Finally, he said, "President Brice is her own person. Everyone has their own unique experiences with life, and hers happened to lead her straight into the White House."

An arm in the front row jutted into the air.

Douglas motioned to the man. The snotty liberal sciences student stood, clearing his throat.

"Professor, I understand that, under the Bush Administration, you were employed by Vertex Labs, which helped design the Albatross warhead bus and delivery system?"

"That is correct," trumpeted Douglas proudly.

The Albatross was one of the first times Douglas was given a top secret security clearance, and he remembered the project well. Warhead placement and accuracy reached an all time high, and the Albatross warheads, made of refined nitrogen particles, could blast furiously while leaving little, if any, radioactive residue.

"At the time we were competing with the new SS-N-18," began the part time weapon's expert. "And that Soviet threat could have easily wiped out an entire state the size of Maryland. It was necessary that we respond with a measured, yet escalated reaction."

"I see!" hissed the student. "And how big of a state could you vaporize with the Albatross? Something the size of Florida? Maybe Texas?!"

Douglas smiled. Another young tendril of Flower Power had sprouted up at his old school. Douglas wasn't surprised, nor affected by the outburst; and as the student was escorted from the hall, he launched into his closing monologue.

"And with the help of men and women like yourselves, we will reach out into new star systems! Our goal is to explore the universe, one parsec at a time! It is this unyielding challenge that will define all generations. Though never conquered, our small and uncertain steps into the Unknown will elevate the human experience. By braving the hostile expanse of space, we push our limits as human beings. And if we continue to do so, we will one day relish in the discoveries and mysteries of the greatest miracle of all."

There was a tired applause.

Douglass graciously acknowledged the scattered kudos.

He couldn't wait to get back to the White House.

# 16

Douglas Rollins landed back at Andrews Air Force Base three hours later, and discovered that everything at his "office" was just as he'd left it.

The White House dinner menu had already been approved, and the carpet cleaners had come and gone. Everything was in complete order, including security procedures. The head of the Secret Service, Jonah Winetraub, a clean-cut graduate out of Stanford, took the next twenty minutes to elucidate his new floor plan and garden sweeps. Twice Doug had stifled a yawn. And a few minutes after lunch he returned to his office feeling ready to face a new challenge. He decided it was *burn time*, time to save the planet from certain doom, something he'd failed to do twice already.

Douglas went to his desk and fingered the keyboard to his Pentium 7000. He didn't need a password with this system, and slipped a 3.5 diskette into the hard-drive. He then leaned back and pressed Enter.

The screen came alive, and the words Jericho! Jericho! appeared in a splash of blinking colors.

Douglas knew, or at least strongly suspected, that there was a clue in the word duplication. There had to be. It would be redundant and irrational to duplicate something unless something triggered a need for the abridgement, a need for the duplication. Everything happens for a reason, and this rule had to apply to this complicated video puzzle. And he also suspected that it was likely to contain an enigmatic epiphany. After all, Jericho! Jericho! made Dungeons and Dragons look like a game of Tic-Tac-Toe.

Electronic data began appearing on the screen, a reminder of the seemingly intractable circumstances involved, and then a voice began to narrate the game, a Vincent Price-like vernacular.

Doug had the Introduction memorized, and wished he could somehow fast-forward to the Solvent Solutions Section.

Then a picture of the Pentagon appeared, and the voice continued to narrate:

*"...and the Secretary of Defense has asked for your help. You will have only three opportunities to solve* Jericho! Jericho! *If you are victorious, you will forever be known as the chosen individual who saved the planet. But if you fail, no one will be known for anything!"*

Douglas typed in his username, *Torah*, and again pressed Enter.

The screen seemed to catch fire as red graphic embers parted and a giant meteor was depicted shooting through space. A tiny representation of the Earth stood in the distance, a blue dot on the plasma screen color monitor.

The narrator continued:

*"The asteroid is moving at* Mach 21, *and its solid core is the size of Alaska. The coaxial center, as well as the mass and circumference, is listed, and the gravitational pull is to be established by the user.*

*"But this is no game.*

*"The asteroid is two-million miles away and closing on a collision course with planet Earth!*

*"All of Mankind's resources are at your disposal!*

*"Good Luck!*

*"And* Torah, *remember, this is your very last chance!"*

A control board of approximately two-hundred icons suddenly appeared. Since the game developed in stages, it was the user's responsibility to address each section as it was presented. The first dealt with aeronautics and aerodynamics, in which the player was instructed to list as many variables and formulas pertinent to the solution. Those involving distance, time, and speed, coupled with reactionary formulas, could be used to complete this section, such as the deployment of a nuclear device designated to stave off the destruction. But since the kiloton or megaton ratio needed to be factored in, along with the means of delivery, mathematical exactitude was critical. The program did the rest.

The computer would ingest the user's solution and look for a comparable match. Jericho! Jericho! was rumored to have only one solvent solution.

But no one really knew.

The scenario was based on genuine scientific data derived from a new Intelleron computer program and Douglas was down to his last strike. Having already tried a cluster of concentrated energy to alter the course of the meteor, as well as detonating a six-megaton warhead on its surface, Douglas decided to try a geometric approach. He was determined to solve the mathematical mystery that some Harvard graduate had alone created.

*Perhaps that kid should have made the meteor smaller,* thought Douglas. *Alaska is a bit much.*

But Douglas remained determined to save the world from the giant meteor. The computer again began to narrate, replaying Doug's fateful error from the last time he played.

And lost.

"As it passed through Jupiter's gravitational pull, it slowed to Mach 11, but your charge of six megatons placed at its center has created an even greater cataclysm! A meteor shower has ensued. Instead of a single meteor the size of Alaska, you've created five the size of Pennsylvania, and did nothing to avert a collision with Earth!

"Your solution is faulty!

"Try Again!"

The Three-D graphics depicted his previous solution with mathematical exactitude, and the meteor was seen splintering.

The solution had to involve accurate placement onto the alien rock, and the ensuing fragments need to somehow be deflected away from the planet.

Like a school of piranha at feeding time, his fingers pecked furiously at the keyboard, employing a defense that he termed *Line of Angels.*

He would employ a powerful and uniquely bold approach.

# 17
# Varanasi, India

The shift started like any other. Junior was talking trash in the transportation room, and several of his cronies were nursing hangovers. Everyone was waiting for the vans that would disperse the teams throughout the various grids.

As Mark punched an electronic time card, he noticed Jerry Tyler stapling a sheet of paper to the bulletin board near the broken coffee machine. Just seconds later, the steward spotted Mark and hurried over.

Jerry was a small guy, with a pointed goatee and narrow brown eyes. He was missing several teeth, and had a tattoo of an Arabian genie winding up his forearm. Something about Jerry reminded Mark of Axle Rose.

"Hey, everybody knows about Junior cleaning you out, Buddy," began the wiry office steward. Tyler was known to run one of the big poker tables on the east side of *Green Village*.

"And we've been keeping an eye on Junior," continued Jerry.

Mark glanced over at the idiot in question. Junior was leaning against a wall locker, steadily annoying someone who was trying to rest. He was wearing that same inane expression he'd worn the night he tossed his markers into the ante, before winding up with all of Mark's savings. Ever since then, Mark felt a sharp lance of disdain whenever he looked at the demolition expert.

"Some guys over on my side of town say Junior has been palming cards on the slide, and dealing from the bottom. And Jake Rollins said the night he went broke, Junior kept reaching for his boot. He thinks he's running an organized hustle. I just thought you might like to know."

Jerry then wandered off, kicking the coffee machine as he passed. "When are they gonna fix this damn thing!"

By nine that morning Mark was on Grid 21, navigating his K-411 across the steep hills. And as he was clearing the southwest corner of the grid, a dark blue Humvee suddenly appeared and rolled onto the clearing. Mark recognized it immediately as belonging to Alvin Torelli, Milton's right hand, his foreman-at-large. A second man was with Torelli, wearing overalls and a baseball cap. The railroad executive began waving at him, and Mark shut of the engine of the dozer and clambered down. As he approached the Humvee, Torelli smiled.

"Tommy Jackson here is going to take over, Mr. Black. He needs to get his feet wet with a Caterpillar. I'll run you back to the village. Get in."

Forgetting to grab his jacket, Mark climbed into the hefty four-wheeler and reached for the seatbelt.

"I was talking to Hickers," began Torelli, wheeling off the grid. "He's very appreciative for your help last night. Have you told anyone at the village about what we found?"

Mark shook his head. "No. I haven't even made it back to my tent yet."

"Good," replied Torelli, smiling crookedly. "Milton would prefer that we keep this between us. He doesn't want a bunch of rumors going around. It could mean bad press, and we don't want that right now."

"Just what did you guys find up there?" asked Mark, turning toward Torelli.

The Italian's eyes narrowed and he looked away. "Nothing of importance. But we don't want these secondary tunnels becoming common knowledge. It could threaten the entire operation, and we don't want that."

Minutes later they wheeled up to Tent Number 4. Mark climbed out of the vehicle.

"You will be paid for the entire shift, Mr. Black" added Torelli through the window. "And Milton has decided to pay you double-time for the time spent with us last night. You were very helpful."

Mark nodded, unsure as to how to thank this mysterious person.

"I really apprec…"

"And remember," interrupted Torelli casually. "No mention of this."

After Torelli's truck rumbled off, Mark stepped inside the tent and went to his bunk. It was unusually quiet, and he realized that he was alone for the first time since coming to India. And, for a second, he didn't quite know how he should act. He went to the Zenith and popped in a tape of last years Super

Bowl.

Torelli gave him the creeps, and Mark began to wonder if there was something more to the story. Was there a connection between Tatiana's unbalanced zeal and Hickers's sudden generosity and caution? Was it a coincidence? Or were these people hiding something?

Mark pushed the conspiracy theory from his mind and tried to get some rest. He dropped into his bunk and draped a towel across his eyes. But Mark couldn't help thinking about what Jerry had said about Junior. It would make perfect sense. Junior was a dirtball, and it wouldn't surprise anyone, especially Mark, if he was getting rich with a loaded deck. Ever since the games had been going on, Junior consistently walked away with the lion's share of winnings.

He'd already sent at least two men straight to the poorhouse.

Mark's eyes wandered to a steel foot locker under Junior's bunk. He probably kept all $12,000 of Mark's money in there. And if Junior was cheating, as everybody seemed to think, then Mark was entitled to get every penny of his losses back, plus interest and a punch in the mouth!

And so was everyone else!

But until there was more proof, he needed to wait. They would be playing cards at Jerry's tonight and Mark decided he would take a mosey over to watch the game firsthand. But then he decided against it. Junior would get wise to the surveillance. There had to be another way.

But his thoughts of Junior were fleeting. He rolled over in bed and began thinking about Tatiana. It was early in the day, and he wondered what she was dong at that very moment.

*Probably stacking rocks or playing with dead things,* he thought with a smile. *My kind of girl. And real sexy, too.*

Even when covered in dirt and perspiration there was something very foreign and exotic about Tatiana. Exciting and mystifying. It was in her Slavic accent, as well as her light blue eyes and pursed lips, lips that seemed to have a dark secret to tell.

*And she'd been locked behind the Iron Curtain,* he thought dryly.

Mark couldn't imagine being told not to pray or go to church. Although he hadn't been to church in years, he didn't understand how one person could exercise that kind of power over another. He felt a distant pang of appreciation for the Red White and Blue.

And then he remembered Tatiana's zealous story about Hittite gods and human sacrifices. He wondered if it would be immoral or dreadfully uncouth to pursue the attractive professional under these trying circumstances, if indeed she was experiencing a mild case of "Jungle Sickness," or some other wacky condition. Did she even find him attractive? With all the American men out working the various grids, why was she showing an openness and interest in him? Was he lucky?

*Ha! Now that's a joke. Judging by the cards Junior tossed me, I don't think luck has shown her face over here.*

Or maybe she was merely using him to get information about Pendleton & Waxler and their progress? He wouldn't be the least bit surprised. Anyone who intercepted radio traffic was cunning and probably well ahead of the game.

Mark decided that it might be a good idea to do a little personal surveillance on Ms. Tatiana Borosky as well as Mr. Junior Jones.

Mark climbed from the bunk and slipped on his boots.

It took thirty minutes to make the walk, and when Mark finally made it to Tatiana's trailer he didn't see her Jeep. He knocked anyway, and after a moment he tried the doorknob. It was unlocked, and Mark stepped slowly into the dark Ranchero, waiting for his eyes to adjust.

"Tatiana? It's Mark! Anybody home?"

As he'd expected there was no reply and Mark decided to wait around in case there was some type of emergency he could help with. He left the door open for additional light and strolled toward the metal desk. Everything appeared to be much as he'd remembered it from earlier that morning. But then he noticed something different. A sheet was covering something in one corner of the Ranchero, and there was a folding chair sitting next to it. The covered object appeared to be some kind of sculpture.

*Perhaps, in her free time, Tatiana is sculpting the face of Everest,* thought Mark, looking for any resemblance in the contours of the hidden work.
*Lord knows she probably needs something to occupy her time. But why is it covered?*

Mark went to the unusual object and reached for a corner of the sheet. He knew artists didn't usually reveal their work until it was completed, but a little looksie wouldn't hurt, especially if she didn't know.

And especially if she wasn't that good.

But before Mark could unveil the object he heard Tatiana's Jeep ratting down the trial. Tatiana wheeled up to the trailer and slammed on the brakes, kicking up clouds of dust. She sprang from the vehicle like a jack-in-the-box, hunching into a combat position and leveling an AK-47 at the Ranchero.

"Come out with your hands up!" she howled. "If you don't show yourself in five seconds I'll open fire! Don't try me! One, Two…!"

"Don't shoot!" cried Mark, stumbling to the doorway. His hands were extended out in front of him. "I just came by to check on you!"

After a glance at the familiar face Tatiana tossed the Russian rifle into the Jeep. She then approached Mark, a look of relief filling her eyes.

"Forgive my concern," she began, removing an ascot scarf from around her neck. "A woman living alone in the jungle has to be careful."

Mark smiled. And at that instant he knew she was not the vulnerable damsel he'd initially presumed. It was quite obvious that Tatiana Borosky could take perfectly good care of herself.

# 18

As Mark hiked slowly back to *Green Village*, ambling along the foothills outside Grid 14, he knew he'd made a fool of himself. Tatiana didn't appreciate his snooping, and Mark felt like he'd gotten a last-minute reprieve. He wanted a quiet dinner alone with Tatiana and, thankfully, he was going to get his chance.

But Mark also remembered that he was flat broke, and again pondered what Jerry had said about Junior. After all, Mark didn't even have the means to cover this upcoming date, something he was really looking forward to. Mark knew a confrontation with Junior was closer than ever, and he began feeling the gradual leak of adrenalin, reminding him of the way he used to feel right before a big test. The butterflies were alive and kicking.

*Udo should be able to lend me a c-note,* he thought with a pang of hope. *That would just about do it. As for Junior, I'll worry about him later.*

But when Mark arrived at the Samsara Club fifteen minutes later, Udo wasn't there, and the third shift partygoers had come and gone. Claw machines sat at ease along the far wall, and a vacant pool table held a clutter of colored balls. Several Indian locals were scattered around, and one man tried selling him a gold watch for ten dollars, while a second tried pedaling a handful of barbiturates. As Mark took a seat at the bar and ordered a beer, a young girl approached, badgering him to buy her a drink.

"Get lost, Sweetie. I'm really busy right now."

The girl began to pout. "But we can have our own little party."

"You belong in school, not a barroom," said Mark, turning away.

"If it isn't Marko-Polo!" came a slurry voice from across the room. Dennis O'Reilly was standing near a broken jukebox, holding a tumbler of whiskey and trying to light a cigarette.

Grabbing his beer, Mark sauntered over.

"They got me, Mark!" spluttered the rig operator. "I don't know how he did it! I was holding a full house, Aces over Fours, and Junior dropped four Kings! He got me for nine-thousand, and my Chase Manhattan credit card."

Mark's mind flashed back to the night he lost his savings. It was four Kings that had beaten him as well.

O'Reilly grabbed the sleeve of Mark's shirt. "Marko, when I thought about it, I later remembered discarding a King! There was no way he could have had four Kings if I discarded one! Impossible! They're a bunch of sharks! I think Junior, McConnel and Atkins are all working together! I don't trust that Junior!"

Mark sighed loudly. "Dennis, I can't believe you gave it all back! I really needed to borrow at least fifty bucks!"

*"I didn't give anything back!"* roared O'Reilly. "I was robbed! And a bunch of us should get together and get our money back!"

"Not tonight," began Mark, trying to think of where he could borrow some money. "I have a pressing appointment. We'll all catch up to him tomorrow, twenty minutes before going on the clock. Be at Tent 4, and tell Jerry when you see him."

"I sure will," cackled Dennis victoriously. He then reached inside a shirt pocket.

He pulled out a crumpled twenty. "This is all I have, Marko, but you can have it. Take it and go in peace."

Mark did, promising to pay it back on the coming Friday. O'Reilly was a godsend, and his conspiracy theory sounded oddly familiar. But for now, Mark decided to stick to Plan A. He bought a bottle of cheap red wine from Arlenta, the middle-aged barmaid, and two carry-out meals. Since the third shift had already been through here, beans and franks were all that remained on the menu. It would have to do. After visiting the showers, Mark raced back to his tent and began to dress. He kept glancing at the footlocker under Junior's bed.

*And now you've got O'Reilly's booty in there, Dynamite Man!*

*Your time is coming, and payback's a bitch.*

Three minutes after slipping on a polo shirt, and a splash from someone's bottle of Old Spice, Mark headed up the trail, balancing two Styrofoam boxes of 'sticks & stones' and a bottle of rock-gut red.

He'd only been gone two hours and even considered waiting in the woods to kill some time. He felt like a teenager going on his first date. The last thing he wanted to do was look too anxious or desperate in front of Tatiana. But he quickly realized just how ridiculous he was beginning to sound.

"Time to grow up, Marko," he mumbled to himself, stumbling through the tall grass.

*She's not going to bite you. Relax and keep your cool.*

He remembered what his sponsor had said about co-dependency. Addicts tend to look for a substitute. And that substitute usually turns out to be sex.

"And make no mistake!" his sponsor had frowned. "You're an addict!"

Mark had a problem with that terminology. Addicts were druggies and drunks. And although he liked to party, he was neither of those. He simply had a little wagering dilemma.

When Mark made it back to the trailer he didn't bother even knocking this time. His arms were full and he was barely able to turn the doorknob, before nudging the door open with his elbow. Wearing a look of accomplishment, he stepped inside the Ranchero, plastic boxes sagging in his arms.

Tatiana had obviously not been expecting company.

The Ukrainian anthropologist sprang out of her chair and lunged toward the desk. Like the strike of a cobra, her hand snatched up a 4-inch box cutter, and for a second her bulging blue eyes were filled with stark terror.

Mark was equally startled and just stood there, not knowing what to say.

Her tension immediately gave way to relief, dropping like the face of an iceberg into the sea. She released the razor, and a trembling hand went to her forehead. "Oh my God. I am too young to have heart attack."

"I'm sorry," said Mark apologetically.

But he was no longer looking at Tatiana. He was gazing at the mound of clay taking shape before him. It was the bust of a creature, something right out of a second-rate Sci-Fi flick. It looked like a lobster with teeth. The thing had a long narrow jaw, like that of a porpoise, and several rows of pointed incisors. It had stalks on its head, like horns, and Mark didn't see anything resembling eyes. He followed the unusual contours, down to the enormous claws dangling toward the floor. Some sort of sharp barbs were affixed to its massive forearms, something that reminded him of a crab.

"I'm flattered," said Mark, smiling. He went to the desk and relieved himself of the trays. "I didn't know you cared."

Tatiana smiled.

After the initial shock wore off, she didn't seem to mind the sudden intrusion. She gazed back at the sculpture, as if staring down a dark tunnel, maybe one of those caves that had gotten everyone so concerned.

"You are probably wondering…"

"I brought us a little something to eat!" broke in Mark, moving to the desk and plopping down the messy cartons. "I wanted to get it here before it got cold."

He again began leering at the hunk of shaped clay.

Her eyes followed his.

"It is not finished," began Tatiana evenly. "But what do you think so far?"

"I think it's scary," said Mark, opening the bottle of wine. "Just what is it supposed to be?"

Tatiana didn't respond. As if she'd forgotten the question, she seemed to be leering into the hidden recesses of her own mind.

"How strong are you?" she finally asked, turning slowly toward him. "Do you have nightmares, Mark Black?"

Now she was starting to freak him out.

*Just a little.*

"No more than the next guy," said Mark casually, trying to untangle his mixed feelings.

"A bust of Julius Caesar, or perhaps Rodin's 'Thinking Man' would have been more appealing," replied Tatiana, sensing his discomfort.

Tatiana began draping her work with the white sheet.

"Wait a minute, Voltaire!" began Mark, not knowing exactly what he meant. "Aren't you going to tell me what it is?"

Tatiana only smiled. "Forgive my dramatic tone, Mark. It has been a very long week."

She glanced at the bottle of wine and stood. "You have been very sweet, and I have been acting like a child. Please accept my apologies."

"No need for apologies," said Mark, moving toward her.

Tatiana spun playfully out of his embrace. "Let me see if I can find something resembling a glass."

# 19
# India

He'd hardly gotten any sleep, and as a new day crept over the *Great Range* Mark rolled onto Grid 16, his dozer freshly fueled from the Second Shift. The dinner date with Tatiana had gone exceptionally well, despite the fact that he didn't get laid. Didn't even get close, in fact. Although they'd stayed up into the wee hours talking, Tatiana effectively countered his subtle advances and playful pawing. But Mark could feel her will cracking, and he estimated that he would probably only need one or two more passes to finally get inside her panties, that is if she even wore panties at all.

Mark was almost certain she didn't.

And to add additional spice to the morning, he could see Tatiana's excavation team on the plateau through the brush, visiting Grid 15.

Again.

Mark studied Tatiana and Ahmel as they ambled across the brush; Tatiana was pointing at the ground, and Ahmel bent down to retrieve something in the mud.

But Mark was not the least bit interested in their archeological quest. He was staring at the tall and sensuous frame of Tatiana, her yellow tank-top revealing generous cleavage, and her long legs, nearly as tall as Ahmel himself, begging for some manly attention. Her buxom physique was a gift to the barren landscape, and he again felt an odd inspiration by her presence.

*Tonight's the night,* he thought, hoping she wouldn't see him staring through the vines like some hard-up adolescent. He then steered the tractor through a dense thicket of *Berrera* vines, feeling almost certain that she was equally attracted to him.

Mark wheeled around and lowered the diesel shovel, charging toward a thicket of *Berrera* like a raging bull. Vines whipped through the air like giant bundles of tumbleweed, and roots and dirt went flying everywhere. Mark deliberately gunned the engine in hopes of getting her attention. Perhaps she could join him for lunch a little later in the day, after she was finished her work.

Maybe even dinner.

And then desert.

*And crazy women are the best in bed.*

As Mark clattered toward another towering mass of vines and trees, deftly maneuvering the giant plow, he never saw the outcropping of granite buried in the underbrush. Halfway into the thicket the iron shovel struck the object with great force, stopping the tractor in its tracks and hurling Mark into the steering levers. The K-411 shrieked in protest, oil now blowing through its topside exhaust. Mark had ruptured something.

Having nearly been shaken out of his skin, Mark killed the engine and sat still for a moment, trying to collect his jangled nerves. Whatever he'd hit was big, and it was deep.

The outcropping was completely cloaked by wild brush and deadwood, but at the tip of his shovel he saw something black and shiny. A wall of vines continued to obscure his view, and Mark clambered down from the K-411. He dropped to the ground and began crawling through the vines. He reached for the object, his gloved hand wiping away the dirt.

He could feel the smooth metallic surface. This wasn't granite, or iron-ore. Although it could prove to be a unique stratum of crystallized onyx, or petrified lava, it wasn't likely. This stuff looked like processed coal, very soft, yet hard as a diamond.

Mark began clearing away the vines with his hands, yanking free the *Berrera* as fast as he could. The object began to take shape, and Mark felt the gnawing pangs of curiosity. Whatever it was, it was only partially exposed, that much he could tell. It appeared to be the tip of something gigantic, and when he looked across its surface he didn't see a single scratch. The shovel of his K-411 hadn't even scratched it.

That wasn't only incredible.

It was nearly impossible.

After clearing away the abstruse "nub," which stood at least five feet fall, he climbed atop the object, still completely puzzled.

"Oh, no! Don't move!" came a harsh whisper from below.

Mark felt his heart leap and looked down. It was Harry Belcher. The fuel truck driver was staring up at him, a startled look on his face and an unlit *Marlboro* clenched between his teeth.

"Do you have any idea what you're sitting on?"

Mark glanced down, smiling. He was looking for any sign of humor in Harry's expression. As usual, there was none.

"No, Belcher. Why don't you tell me what I'm sitting on?"

The man cleared his throat and spoke in a low, conspiring tone. "You happen to be planted on the only missile silo in India! It's pointed straight for Pakistan and its got a hair trigger! Any false moves and you'll set it off!"

Jack felt a wash of relief and began climbing down from the iron horn. Belcher was a joke a minute, and you just never knew what would be coming out of his mouth.

"But seriously," began Mark, wiping his grimy brow. "It's probably from the 17th Century, or something. When the Brits were here. Tatiana, that geologist, found a bunch of British shit over on 15. A canon, some torn uniforms, and human bones."

"It seems to be made of steel or some other metal," observed Belcher, trudging through the brush and reaching for the horn. "It's definitely been manufactured."

"Probably a church bell," rejoined Mark, remembering something Tatiana had told him. "Believe me, after the Brits left in 1947, the Hindus trashed everything and anything Anglo. For all we know, that could be one of the Queen Mum's fancy carriages down there."

"Yea," replied Belcher, chuckling nervously. "Or maybe the dreadnought *HMS Britain.*"

The men enjoyed a laugh as an arid wind began blowing down from the mountain, sending a veil of dirt whipping across the grid. The gale was strong and swept branches and leaves into a giant funnel, before dispersing as quickly as it had come. The sun had begun its descent behind the towering glacier, and dark veils of shadow began creeping across the land of *Borabi.*

Mark then noticed Tatiana and Ahmel fast approaching in theJeep. They had obviously heard the collision and must have noticed him climbing down from the tractor. But as theJeep wheeled up and the digging-duo climbed out, Mark wasn't thinking of the soft tread of Tatiana's Birkenstock sandals, her generous breasts, or her long, shapely legs.

He smiled, however, and thought:

*So just what in the hell was I sitting on?*

# 20

"We dug up an Italian tank in Ethiopia once," began Tatiana softly, running her hand across the smooth metallic surface. They'd cleared most of the vines away, and everyone was gazing absently at the pointed object. Tatiana was convinced that it was just what she'd been searching for, and could feel the adrenalin pumping through her veins now. She did her best to remain calm.

"The tank crew was still inside," continued the scholar distractedly. "Which is probably why they were known as mobile coffins."

Tatiana again reached for the alloy. "But Mother Nature eventually claims everything."

Ahmel continued deepening a trench around the object, his spade working furiously. Pierce had already called the equipment manager, and waited patiently as a repairman was brought out.

What Mark didn't know was that Junior was on his way out, also.

Tatiana then got on her cell-phone, trying to sound calm and collected. And although she'd turned away, Mark could hear her every word, her choppy Slavic tones heated and terse.

"Artonus, this is Tatiana. I need you up here with the carbon testing equipment. We do not have much time."

Then, after a pause, her voice sharpened.

"Fine! I will attempt to send a sample to Delhi for testing. But I do not know why you are making my life so *diffecuwt*!"

She terminated the call and resumed staring at the unusual object.

"Just what do you think it is?" asked Mark, moving toward her.

Tatiana shrugged. "I honestly do not know. Nor could I estimate how long it has been here. A few hundred years, maybe."

Junior appeared on the trail seconds later, wheeling onto the grid with a truckload of dynamite stuffed inside his cabin.

105

"Where's Fred Flintstone?" chortled the demolition expert, climbing from his pick-up. "I heard all about the trouble."

Junior turned to Tatiana, a gleam in his eye and a fork in his tongue. "Wanna watch me turn Fred Flintstone into Barney Rubble?"

Junior was a salacious bastard with little moral restraint, and Mark stepped between them. "We're gonna have a little talk later, buddy boy."

Junior ignored him. "Aren't you going to introduce me to the beautiful woman, Marko Polo? After all, I'm only a working stiff doing his job."

Junior didn't take the bait, and Mark sighed heavily.

"Tatiana, meet Junior. He's Pendleton & Waxler's demolition man."

"Very pleased to meet you," chortled Junior affectionately, his work temporarily forgotten.

"All right, Don Juan," broke in Mark. "Now you're holding me up."

Although Mark's tone rang with jest and sarcasm, there was an underlying trace of genuine contention, and more than a little disdain. Mark was really feeling it now. The beautiful Slavic scholar was out of Junior's league, and Mark was going to see that it stayed that way.

*His dick is probably still wet from some teenager last night.*

Mark didn't know why he was feeling the way he was. He wasn't necessarily thinking about getting laid, not necessarily, and he had absolutely no connection whatsoever to this woman. Technically, she was fair game.

But Mark felt almost as if he were protecting a sister or niece, rather than the honor of some matron. He felt the need to shield Tatiana from the likes of Junior.

Junior Jones was bad news.

"I thought I'd seen all the beauty these mountains had to offer," continued Junior smiling. He was holding a bundle of dynamite and connecting some wires. Tatiana watched him with an air of curiosity.

"But I had obviously missed the most beautiful of visions," continued Junior, looking up and winking.

Mark was suddenly standing between them again.

"You're gonna be seeing beautiful things through a black eye if you don't move it, Junior!"

As if coming out of a dream, Junior finally got the point. He smiled at Mark before walking slowly toward the exposed hull of the ship.

"Touchy today, eh, Mark?" he muttered, more to himself. "Shallow pockets tend to do that."

Using duct tape, Junior strapped the charge around the horn and sauntered back to his truck. When everyone was clear, he broke into a stupid smirk and triggered the device. This blast was low in nitroglycerine, and not as magnificent as the others; but the blast sent a sharp shockwave belting across the grid. A funnel of dirt rose up, and a shower of clay rained down seconds later.

And when the smoke cleared, everyone was staring in disbelief.

# 21

When he got the news Milton Hickers was sitting at a long refractory table in his office. Three representatives from India's House of the People were with him, their briefcases and cellular phones scattered loosely around the long table. Milton was not in the mood for a debate, or a plea for economic concessions. Not today. Since he'd been here his blood pressure was up twenty points, and he felt himself cracking under the pressure of the Orient Express II. And he didn't like what he was beginning to hear from hushed voices in Delhi.

*And now these jokers are here!*

"I want to thank you for taking the time to meet with us this morning, Mr. Hickers," began one young assistant, Entuo something or another. "And I fully realize that you are currently preoccupied with your manifold duties surrounding this operation."

Milton grunted. "And what can I help you with?"

A second assistant from Delhi removed a stack of photographs from his briefcase. "We did not want to bring the police, because of the negative connotations. After all, there has not yet been a crime committed, and all of this may be an elaborate misunderstanding."

"We certainly hope so," added the first man.

"We would like to know if you or any of your men have seen these missing persons?"

The Indian official laid the photos on the table before Milton. Hickers scooped them up.

"We do not know if the youths became involved in prostitution and frequented the local taverns," one of the men explained. "Some visual identification would be very helpful at this stage."

"Just what do you want me to do?" asked Milton, shuffling through the pictures. There were at least thirty of them. "It's the world's oldest profession."

"Yes, but these children never made it home. Some of them have been missing for three weeks, and we are beginning to consider a more sinister possibility."

Milton looked up, and quickly removed his reading glasses. "Just what are you implying? Do you think someone in my company has something to do with this? Like Ted Bundy, or Son of Sam?"

"We are not accusing anyone of anything, but…"

"Good!" interrupted Milton. "Because I do a thorough criminal background checks on everyone that works with my railroad."

"We are not here to point fingers or make accusations," intoned Enduoto. "We are simply looking for a little cooperation."

Milton leaned back in his chair. "I'm listening."

"Just distribute these photographs to all of your employees," continued Enduto. "Maybe hang them in the tents, or in the crew cafeteria. We are hoping someone comes forward with some information. Their parents are an emotional mess."

"That won't be a problem," said Milton reaching for the telephone. "And I'll go one better."

Milton was going to hand these gentlemen to Mary Bartlett in accounting. She was a good listener and would keep these men occupied long enough for him to slip back out to Grid 35. Lechler had said they'd discovered another tunnel, and Milton thought he was beginning to lose his mind.

But even before he had a chance to dial the number, a radio atop his desk crackled to life. Milton reached for the Motorola and turned to the men. "Excuse me, gentlemen."

"Hickers here!" he grumbled.

"We have a problem, Milton."

Everyone in the room could hear the exchange, and Milton turned away, like a Chinese dragon nestled on a perch.

"What are you talking about, Brummer?"

"Grid 16 clearing. We've hit a roadblock, quite literally. At first we thought it was a giant lump of nickel, or iron ore, or some other heavy alloy blocking our path. But something big is standing in our way, over."

"First you find bones, and now more rocks! Blow it out, Brummer!"

"We tried," continued the voice. "In fact, we've blown all around it, and this is beginning to look like the hull of a ship. A steel ship. But there are no signs of rivets or seams of any sort."

Milton's eyes narrowed into tiny slits, and his mouth opened, resembling both a smile and a grimace. A wheezy laugh began to fill the air as Milton Hickers chuckled.

"And now you are finding ships in the Himalayas! Do you suspect it might be *Noah's Ark*? How about the *Edmund Fitzgerald?* Have we located any German U-boats out here yet? And don't forget the Voltaire-Buffon thingie!"

There was a pause and the foreman didn't seem to acknowledge the sarcasm.

"You really have to see this thing, Milton."

# 22
# India

*Holy mother of God!*

It was sticking out of the ground like the rhino-horn of Everest itself, with a long connecting hump near the dirt line. A group of at least a dozen men were standing around the unusual cynosure, trying to figure out just what in the hell could be buried beneath one of their grids.

Milton climbed from his shiny Dodge *Ram* and stared in amazement. It did indeed appear to be some kind of ship.

*Just what else could it be?*

"Black struck it with a K-411," called Junior from the crowd. "Knocked the tractor out of commission and didn't scratch that thing."

Someone else was standing on the hump now. "Can't see a rivet or seam. It's almost as if it were cast from a mold. Smooth as glass."

Lechler was there as well, heading the ad hoc excavation. "We tried everything imaginable to cut into it. Nothing worked. Welding torches, power saws, titanium drill bits, and explosives. Nothing even scratched the surface. Nothing."

"It's not even warm to the touch," began a First Shift mechanic. "It absorbs heat, and it's stronger than Kevlar."

"What does it look like Althoff?" groaned Milton, turning to his geological engineer.

Wayne Althouff was already busy assembling a computer terminal with a color monitor. He began plugging up cables to an electric generator. "I dunno. But we can find out just how big it is."

The engineer was preparing to detonate a small explosive which would create a shock-wave reading. The seismic gauge resembled a shotgun, and operated on a similar premise. A cartridge of black powder was inserted into the breech, and a trigger activated the firing pin, which detonated the charge. The charge was shot into the ground, and the returning seismic waves were depicted on the computer monitor. It was a form of subterranean radar.

Althoff detonated the very concentrated charge and gazed at the color monitor. Although they couldn't feel the ground shake, the concussion shot waves deep into the Earth's crust, and when they returned an image was depicted on the computer monitor.

A splash of wavy lines appeared across the screen, and Althoff began shaking his head.

"Milton, this thing is enormous."

Hickers approached the monitor as Althoff continued:

"It's the size of a football field!"

Milton shifted his gaze back to the hump in the dirt.

"How are you going to get it out, Althouff?" asked Milton, his blood pressure rising.

"There is no getting it out. We'll have to go around it."

"Or somehow cut it in half," surmised a structural engineer. "Maybe go through it."

Milton flashed a grimace. "Then why are you still standing here?!"

# 23

When Mark finally made it back to *Green Village* it was cool and quiet. A mellow breeze whipped gently through the tent, and a distant snore ambled lazily through the damp air. Mark was totally drained and knew it wouldn't take long before he was sound asleep. The exhausted heavy equipment operator eased his tired body into the bunk before staring into the recesses of his mind.

It was the craziest day Mark could ever remember, and he would never forget the expression on Milton's face as they tried to identify the object on Grid 16. They'd managed to unearth much of its topside, and when Mark left with the others Milton was just beginning to bring in the heavy excavation equipment.

Feeling deflated from all the excitement, Mark fell quickly asleep thinking about distant stars and alien races. Tatiana had one hell of an imagination, but he had to admit that a lot of what she said was beginning to make sense. The universe, its size, age and composition, was capable of birthing just abut anything imaginable, and Mark felt a tweak of discomfort when he tried to consider the religious implications.

Mark often pondered the universe and its many untold secrets, and there was little doubt in his mind that other forms of life existed elsewhere. Otherwise, it would be an enormous waste, and the Creator wasn't wasteful. Besides, the aggressive nature of Nature, another of His creations, seemed to dictate it.

But what if there were "others" who didn't acknowledge or recognize a Higher Power, those who didn't understand, or couldn't comprehend, the premise of the Ten Commandments, who'd never heard of the Supreme God who gave of his only Son so that we may be given eternal life? Or so the story went. What if they cared nothing for moral fabric, and relied strictly on the base instincts concerning survival?

Perhaps there were planets where their own versions of Hitler and Tojo had won the great wars. That alone would constitute a moral conduct and fiber vastly different from our own.

Moral absenteeism.

Complete spiritual malfeasance.

Now that was a scary thought.

# 24

*"Aces over Kings!"* a voice barked out. "And Daddy wins another one!"

The words belted through the air like a jackhammer, and Mark didn't even have to open his eyes to now that Junior and the others were at it again. The television was blaring with last year's Super Bowl and curtain of cigarette smoke wafted through the tent. Mark heard someone crushing an empty beer can.

*"Full House!"* barked Junior moments later, slamming down his cards onto the table. "And I'll take that!" he added, raking in another substantial ante.

Mark was surprised that Jones was here. But when he thought about it, it wasn't too unusual, especially if he'd found out that Jerry and the others had gotten wise to his five-card scam.

*So he decided to return to the scene of the crime!* thought Mark, climbing from his bunk to prepare a cup of instant coffee. *The place where it all began! Like an arsonist who wants to admire his evil handiwork.*

Mark realized it would be the perfect time to watch Junior. He was drunk, and he would get sloppy.

"Looks like they're thinking about a little excavation," began someone at the table. Mark didn't recognize the man. He was tall and lean, and wearing a Pittsburgh Steelers cap.

*Another unsuspecting newcomer,* thought Mark. *Fresh meat!*

"Well, they better be all finished by the time Lechler gets there," commented Junior. "He'll bury those geologists in cement before stopping."

"Maybe that thing is a Martian spacecraft," began Henry Ratliff, an unskilled laborer with P&W. Ratliff was a big kid with an oafish expression, someone Mark knew wasn't in Junior's card scam.

After a new hand was dealt, Junior tossed a twenty into the pot, and several players folded immediately. Jake Brenner met the Twenty and raised the bet, tossing two more Twenties into the ante. Ratliff concurred, and Junior looked uncertain, gazing absently at his cards.

Mark was watching him closely now from across the tent. And he saw Junior's hand slip casually off the table, before dropping between his legs.

"I just sent home some pictures of that mountain," began Ratliff. "It sure is something to look at."

"K2 is right down range," someone was saying. "Damn near every bit as big."

"What are you gonna do, Junior?" asked the newcomer, peering over the tops of his cards.

But rather than producing another winning hand, Junior casually folded, and his eyes darted right to Mark.

He knew he was being watched, and smiled.

"Hey, Marko, did you roll that communist broad yet?"

Mark felt as if he'd been slapped. Junior was leering from behind a beer can, his other hand jingling some loose change atop the table.

It was time. And it had been a long time coming. Mark remembered something Tatiana said about crossing the Rubicon. Well, Junior had done just that. There would be no turning back.

But Mark would not be facing Junior alone today. Before he could even throw the first punch, five other men stepped into the tent and began circling the card table. Faces were partially covered with hoodies, but Mark instantly recognized one of the men.

"Where's the money?" began Jerry Thornton, wrapping a strap of leather around his bony fist.

"What in the hell are you talking about?" flared Junior, dropping his beer and bolting to his feet.

"Boy, we can do this the easy way, or we can take the long road!" hissed Jerry, stepping closer. "It's all up to you, Fat Boy."

"Go fuck yourself!" flared Junior. "I beat every last one of you fair and square!"

They would be the last words he spoke in a long time.

# 25
# Grid 59
# Six Miles South Of Nepal

They made the gruesome discovery as *Husquavarna* chain saws ripped and riddled the moist air. The modern-day lumberjacks were spread out over a three mile radius, their chain saws and limb-chippers roaring aloud, spitting sawdust and belching streams of purple smoke. Less than a hundred yards behind them, and rolling along a low ridge, were two Caterpillar K-411s. The dozers were clattering slowly toward the saw men, a field of felled trees between them. The first dozer roared thunderously, before tipping a rotten stump onto its side and pushing it toward a small clearing; the second K-411 clattered toward a felled oak, mashing a carpet of branches and vines as it approached.

But the first tractor suddenly stopped, and the driver began gunning the engine. One of its tracks had become stuck in the ground. As the steel belt began spinning, the earth shifted dramatically and the dozer slipped further into the crevice, tilting dangerously and nearly tipping over. The operator flipped the tracks into reverse and mashed the accelerator. More dirt began flying through the air, but the tractor only sank deeper, a dense root system barely keeping the K-411 from tumbling completely into the camouflaged ravine.

The tractor suddenly stalled out, and a wall of dirt collapsed beneath it, revealing the immense cavern.

"Holy Christ!" muttered the dozer operator.

No one wanted to inform Milton of another roadblock, at least not until it had been thoroughly investigated, and Bernie Coleman, a geological surveyor for P&W Construction, volunteered to head the investigation.

As Bernie fastened a thick leather belt to his shoulder harness, a cable was clipped to a metal ring on his vest. Other than a hardhat, Bernie wore a cotton mask which covered his mouth and nose, something to offset the awful stench wafting up from the hole in the ground, and a radio was clipped to his harness.

"You ready, Bernie?" someone called from the electric winch.

"All set!" barked Coleman, flipping a thumbs-up.

Hefting a powerful spotlight, he was slowly lowered into the hole, his light sending a myriad of shadows shimmering across the black walls. The crevice seemed bottomless at first, an no light was reflected off the bottom. But as he descended down into the cavern, gliding silently into darkness, Coleman began to hear the echoed chirping.

"See anything yet, Bernie?" a voice crackled over his radio.

Bernie swung around on the rope and pressed the radio's transmit button.

"Nothing yet, but I hear something. It sounds like a bird chirping."

Bernie was lowered another fifty feet, and a group of workers began gathering around the mouth of the cave. Everyone had been expecting something unusual to emerge, something incredible, but an enormous underground cavern was not what many had expected.

As Bernie reached the 180-foot mark, he began to see something on the ground below.

"I think I see the bottom!" called Coleman into his radio.

And as his Halogen light danced across the floor of the cave, Bernie thought he'd entered some ungodly corner of hell. He could now see the mounds of debris, and the stench was almost palpable. He realized that he was looking at cairns of bones. He had been lowered into a stench-ridden mausoleum, an ocean of death, some ungodly holocaust of destruction. The human remains were piled high, thousands of years of death amassed in one charnel, a sprawling and rancid necropolis.

"Stop! Stop lowering me!" cried Bernie.

The electric winch suddenly stopped, and Bernie was dangling only ten feet from the rancid peaks.

"Guys, you dropped me into hell! It's filled with corpses and bones! It's like a massive dumping ground for the dead. Get me out of here!"

"Can you see anything else?" crackled a voice, echoing through the cavern. "Any connecting tunnels or other means of access?"

Bernie wasn't listening. He was watching the shifting shadows below. Something was moving, and it was moving toward him.

"I see something moving down here!" shrieked Bernie. "Pull me up guys! Hurry and pull me up!"

Another figure shambled out of the darkness and stumbled over the blanket of bones; and then another. Bernie began to hear the chirping, the loud shrieks of a hungry bird or animal. Then they began jumping, trying to grab his dangling legs, giant arms swinging below him.

Something touched his boot, and Bernie began kicking his feet wildly. He suddenly felt something grab his boot, and there was a stab of pain in his foot. "Pull me the fuck up! Hurry! *Ahhhhh...!*"

With a sharp tug, the winch began spinning, hoisting the tortured geologist from the horrid shadows.

Bernie dropped his light, and stared down as it tumbled into the darkness...

...as it tumbled into hell.

# 26
# United Nations Headquarters
# Along the East River
# New York City

She was sitting in an adjoining office, wearing a smart blue business suite and a brooch given to her by her mother. With the silver swan gracing her lapel, the President tried her best not to blink. She felt like she was getting a haircut in an old fashioned barbershop, like the one she visited as a child with her grandfather. Tess had an apron draped across her shoulders, and her head was tilted slightly back.

Someone was applying powder to her cheeks. Then they began brushing her nose with additional mask.

"It will help if you start to perspire," the make-up person said. "The additional lights can get uncomfortably warm."

Tess only smiled. But the President was using the time to revamp her presentation.

*Best to go straight from the hip,* she thought, remembering the escalation between the United States and North Korea. She'd addressed this very same assembly two weeks before the United States declared war on the rogue Asian nation, before her predecessor launched a storm of Tomahawk cruise missiles across the 38th Parallel. The North Korean dictator had gotten his wish: individual talks with the United States concerning nuclear proliferation, *mano-a-mano.* And when those talks broke down, Contessa Brice, then heading the *NSA,* glared boldly across the Pacific Ocean.

And she didn't blink.

Today, she would address the representatives of the General Assembly in much the same way her Republican predecessor had, only now she was wielding some leverage.

After the landings at Wonsan and Inchon, and after occupation forces rounded up nearly one-hundred North Korean civilians and herded them into the Hague to be charged with war crimes, the world's pessimism concerning a rapid conclusion of hostilities became centered on how to rebuild the shattered Sinic nation.

Therefore, the upcoming discussions, which would be mired with political altercations, were really more of a business meeting rather than a rallying cry for democracy. The war was over. And her approach, modeled on that of Alexander the Great, meant that the U.N. had become her Gordian Knot, something to be "circumvented" in times of high political duress and diplomatic erosion.

And the added stress of being the first woman to lead a superpower through the wake of battle did little to dampen her resolve. She was well aware that the entire world was watching, and that every female and minority from Cape of Good Hope to New York City studied her with heightened awareness.

And they would see a strong woman.

Not only the speedy resolution of combat in North Korea, but her missile defense system, as well as her child-care incentives and educational package would become the pedestals upon which would rest her legacy, a legacy that every generation, whether black or white, red or yellow, would come to admire and respect.

President Brice had made those goals clear during her campaign run, stating, "Unlike some of my predecessors, I will not just throw money at a problem. And there is a difference between a hand-out and a hand-up. Welfare should not be a lifestyle, but an augmentation through tough times and unfortunate circumstances. We all have had bad things happen to us and need a little help from time to time. But the U.S. Government should never go into the business of childrearing. The White House and Capitol Building are not nurseries! Besides, we have our own families to raise!"

Her point was clear.

And her approval rating reflected it.

But the nations represented in the General Assembly weren't concerned with budget cuts or food stamp programs. They wanted to discuss the international stage, something Contessa was equally prepared to delineate.

*Besides, I was overdue for a trip to New York.*

Her address lasted 23 minutes, three minutes longer than she'd scripted, and that's because she decided to underscore the importance of a democratic North Korea. The world was still in a fray over the Second Korean War and, as Contessa had expected, Russia and China were opposed to a prolonged American occupation of the defeated communist nation.

*And that is all fine and good*, she thought as she boarded *Air Force One* for her return flight to Washington. *But the victor in war writes the rulebook.*

# 27

When President Brice returned to the White House she fell back into her schedule with a disciplined ease. Her very first meeting was with Homeland Security advisor Robert Ridge, scheduled for the very same day she returned from New York. The top-level security administrator briefed her on the preventive and Intelligence aspects of the ongoing war on Terror, including implementation of the new airline facial-recognition cameras currently being tested at terminals around the country. The science was sensible and very effective. Facial structure, features, and dimensional aspects were analyzed by a computer, and if they matched any of the five-thousand suspected terrorists in the computer banks, a red flag was issued across the site. It was all a part of her new Eastern Terror Initiative.

"*Hamas* is always plotting something," began Ridge, scanning a CIA memo. "We're getting unusually heavy traffic from Pakistan to Damascus. But we are also getting a deluge of intense cellular traffic throughout India and surrounding areas. We think something unusual is afoot."

Tess thought about the cell-phone intercepts. It was ironic how much information the terrorists would convey across the ether. If you used Western technology, you were subject to the rules of the West.

And as President Contessa Brice continued to be briefed, something altogether different was boiling out of control in India.

No one could have imagined that, in less than two weeks time, she would convene with these very same individuals, only then the circumstances would warrant a Defcon 1 Alert, placing the nation on a footing for total war.

It would be something no President, past or present, would have ever expected to encounter, something that made the Cuban Missile Crisis seem like a playground quarrel.

After meeting at length with the Speaker of the House, to whom her

Welfare Reconstruction Plan was better clarified, Tessa returned to the Oval Office to meet with her Joint Chiefs as well as the Secretary of Defense.

Melvin Knoll was wearing his customary scowl, but his voice was open and genial.

"After the initial trial runs we should have partial deployment by 2012," began the czar of defense.

Knoll was seated before her desk, legs crossed, hands resting atop his lap, their fingers tightly laced. "Abe thinks he will be ready for the next phase of testing by the middle of next month. I'm beginning to think he's finally got the right recipe."

Secretary Knoll had the President's full attention.

The nation's missile defense system had become known as the Hades Project. It was a high-speed interceptor system comprising the new Northrop/ Grumman Mark 50 high altitude ICBM interceptors. Having survived the Cold War without such a defense, America was suddenly on the verge of a cost-efficient and reliable counter-measure to incoming enemy missiles, something that would effectively abandon the insane philosophy of Mutual Assured Destruction, something Tess was very eager to accomplish. This was her vanguard campaign proposal, and she kept the issue in the Press and very much on her political "front burner." And although the Cold War had gone the way of the dinosaur, a new and asymmetrical threat was rising, something that required an asymmetrical response. After all, the nation had just waged a war over it.

As Melvin withdrew a stack of photographs from his briefcase, the President stood and sauntered toward Secretary Knoll. She felt at ease discussing the new weapon's system, especially with Melvin, and had grown accustomed to the technical jargon surrounding such projects.

She only wished Congress was more receptive. Tess had barely squeaked the project's first one-hundred billion dollar appropriation through the Senate, yet another vote was to take place in several months, a pivotal vote which would either ensure the eventual deployment of Hades, or give it a decent burial.

But, despite the program's declining support, Tess could not be swayed to back away from Hades. Indeed, the missile defense system had become her cornerstone in the Presidential campaign, especially after 2006, and it was going to remain her primary initiative.

And her reasoning was sound.

Providing the trigger to the Second Korean War was the North Korean acquisition and testing of Chinese Silkworm missiles, all armed with a broad range of tactical "nukes." The Eastern Axis of Evil was suddenly in possession of five such warheads, coupled with a reliable and functional means of delivery. The Silkworms represented the new epitome of tactical nuclear weapons, and her predecessor had put it down with an iron fist. The logic was sound, since one nuclear Silkworm could wipe out an entire American fleet.

Indeed, missile defense became her top priority, even though many Democrats voted against the bill, citing that Korea's swift, yet brutal, incapacitation rendered the threat impotent. But, as far as Tess was concerned, the threat was always palpable and real.

The rules were changing.

Although still in the research and development stage of development, early results were promising.

And, as Knoll had stated, Hades was ready to begin a new phase of testing.

At the conclusion of the briefing, as Melvin summoned his driver and prepared to return to the Pentagon, President Brice gazed at the Hades hard-copy atop her polished desk. The words *Top Secret: Secretary's Copy* were emblazoned across the front of the document.

Tess opened the file and gazed down at the name listed at the top of the lengthy report.

To herself, she pronounced the typewritten name.

*Abraham Rosenblum.*

# 28
# Mustang, Nepal

As Fuzi Verdo loaded the last of the furniture, rolling a wet loveseat and recliner into the back of his Chevy Blazer, the sky continued to grow overcast and stormy. After tossing the torn cushions into the back of his truck, Fuzi jumped quickly behind the wheel and started the worn-out engine. A cool wind was sweeping down from Mount Everest, rustling the banks of *Berrera* vines as it whispered a warning of rain. Fuzi could not ignore the approaching weather system and quickened his pace, driving a few meters up the dirt road where two mattresses had been tossed into an adjoining alley. The many surrounding hovels and corrugated steel shanties clustered along the Nepalese sierra housed people that could best be described as acutely impoverished.

The inhabitants of northern *Borabi* were primarily fringe dwellers, social outcasts who'd managed to create their own wretched subculture and social caste; and it was Fuzi's job to clean after them.

After tossing the flimsy mattresses onto a tangle of bicycle frames, Fuzi's eyes drifted to an abandoned GE washing machine and a pair of broken dining room chairs. Two children suddenly burst into laughter as they scampered past, their piercing shrieks sending a finger of discord running along Fuzi's spine, fingernails on a chalkboard.

Realizing that he could always return tomorrow, and feeling the aches of a stiff back, Fuzi decided to pass on the appliances and returned to his truck, lighting a Turkish cigarette and coughing wheezily.

His eyes rolled slowly across the stark horizon. But he wasn't studying the rolling hills of *Berrera;* he was looking for the young prostitute he frequently occasioned. Finally noticing the door to her shanty closed, and the curtains tightly pulled, Fuzi sighed dejectedly before rolling off into the countryside, navigating the dirt roads like a safari scout through the Congo.

The extended bed of his pick-up truck was haphazardly framed with tall sheets of plywood, increasing his load capacity. But the Chevy was well beyond its hauling capacity, with discarded appliances and broken furniture piled high all around him; and the rear of the truck hung low, its axle struggling at maximum capacity.

Fuzi mashed the clutch and shifted gears, his bumper barely grazing the ground as he rolled deeper along the bumpy trail. In the distance shimmered the white horn of Everest, its frosted peak disappearing into the gray roll of clouds.

There was nothing back here, nothing but an ocean of twisted *Berrera* vines and accumulated junk.

Fuzi rolled about five miles into the sprawling underbrush, and on several occasions he thought he saw something moving in the thickets and bramble along the trail. His eyes kept glancing at the thick walls of vines, and he could not shake the uncanny sensation that he was being followed.

It began to cool, and Fuzi could smell the damp scent of coming rain. As his truck labored through the deep compost and thick underbrush, a flash of lightning hissed across the blanket of gray, forking wildly toward the ground. Fat droplets of rain suddenly began spattering his windshield, and a foreboding wind began whirling down from the body of Everest, the frosted matterhorn now completely invisible in the rolling clouds.

Fuzi decided to stop right here. He'd gone far enough. Although the junk man usually preferred taking a load deeper into the valley, now was not the time to be doing it. With heavy rains coming, the compost would soon be transformed into a mud pit, nearly impossible to navigate, and Fuzi remembered that he might be getting low on fuel. Although his fuel gauge was broken, he'd already been out here twice that afternoon. With heavy rains on the way, this was scheduled to be his last load of the day.

And the last load of his life.

Fuzi climbed from his truck and went to the tailgate. Without a pause he hurled the twin mattresses into the vines, and then sent an air-conditioner crashing through the thick foliage, tumbling end-over-end into the valley.

But as Fuzi reached for the busted *Zenith* television, he heard something, the rustle of dead vines. He then glimpsed something moving in the brush beneath him. He couldn't make out what was approaching, perhaps a raccoon or capybara, something known to flourish here. But when he saw the flash of giant teeth, he knew he was in big trouble.

It was a savage bite, cutting through his boot and shattering the tiny bones in his foot. With an ungodly shriek, large mandibles sank into his other *Brahma* boot, and Fuzi screamed as teeth pierced his metatarsal.

The junk man cried out, kicking wildly at the *Berrera;* but the creatures had vanished back into the underbrush.

*Mountain lions*, he thought frantically, reaching for his bloody boot.

But these teeth had left an impression unlike any other.

As Fuzi hobbled toward his truck, he could hear it moving in the vines behind him. And he then realized that the creatures were not alone. He could suddenly hear them moving through the underbrush all around him, their enormous heads bobbing through the growth as they ambled clumsily along the uneven ground.

The sky grew dark and tiny black orbs occasionally appeared through the vines, elongated eyeballs poking through the stalks of *Berrera.* Fuzi's heart began racing, allowing the venom to move quicker into his bloodstream.

Fuzi would leave the couches by the roadside, not bothering to send them tumbling into the *Berrera* vines. They would be an eyesore and he would probably get a reprimand; but he didn't care. He could barely walk and he could feel his lower leg becoming inflamed; he needed to get to a doctor immediately.

*And something is following me!*

Fuzi slung open the door to his truck and collapsed into the driver's seat. His vision was blurry, and his mouth was dry as a bone. He hadn't yet started the engine when the dirt road began undulating, his pupils now fully dilated. Fuzi could almost feel the blood swishing through his veins, could feel the deep nausea sweeping across him.

Then the *Berrera* vines came alive.

Fuzi fumbled with his key chain. He could hear the vines being ripped loose as they lumbered toward him, tracking their human quarry like giant vultures. Then he could hear them chattering, their screechy voices astir with excited cackles and chirps.

*They are communicating!* Fuzi thought wildly. *They are talking about me!*

And then the enormous claws appeared at his window, reminding Fuzi of a giant stone crab. His head was swimming with venom now, and he wasn't sure if he was hallucinating. But the eyes staring through his windshield sent his heart into cardiac arrest. The tiny orbs watched him patiently, a vulture on the stalk.

*Dear God! Am I imagining things?*

He'd heard the stories, the tales going back as far as his family could remember. But this was supposed to be folklore!

Fuzi started the engine, his arm now burning painfully. Tools spilled onto the road as he slipped the gear into Drive.

*What in God's name is happening?*

His mind suddenly flashed back. As a child Fuzi remembered the terrible incident that had taken place here. The many people, their butchered bodies found buried in the brush. Men, women and children crying for their loved ones. And then he remembered what the local tribesman had said.

Seconds later Fuzi lost consciousness, and his truck rolled slowly into an embankment of *Berrera* and vanished, the glow of its tail lights swallowed up.

They quickly surrounded the truck, scurrying through the vines like overweight monkeys.

Then they began to devour him.

# Book II

# Unknown Sciences

# 29
# Varanasi, India

When it was finally over he had a severe concussion and would need eighteen stitches and over thirty staples. Junior's jaw had been fractured in two places, and his eyes were swollen shut, rising like puff-pastries in the oven. Three ribs had been cracked as well, and the doctor said he would be lucky if he ever regained full use of his right eye.

And as Junior was wheeled out of *Green Village* in an ambulance, his escorts raided his bank account, cashing a flurry of checks with each of their names affixed. Junior didn't give in without a fight. As they rifled through his footlocker and went through every inch of his truck, the demolition expert began to resist, and the lights went out in a hurry. And when the masked men found no cash, they began beating their host into submission.

And then Junior passed out.

*And he'd done it to himself,* thought Mark, remembering the pool of blood in the dirt.

Although they never found an Ace in his boot, or a King up his sleeve, they no longer needed to. The multiple coincidences, the laws of average and the scattered rhetoric was enough to incite the rebellion.

But there was another catalyst for the violent reaction, something far more complicated than a dirty dealer, something that also affected livelihoods, on a much grander scale, and even warranted vigorous union intervention.

It was the sudden cancellation of rail operations.

The Orient Express II had stalled.

When Monday morning came pink slips appeared atop bunk-beds, informing the men of the indefinite layoffs, and when the railroad didn't immediately comment on the sweeping layoffs, tempers flared. Thousands of union members were suddenly out of work and many returned angrily to Delhi to await a flight back to the States. But a few remained in *Varanasi,* convinced that the cessation was only temporary.

But within a matter of days *Varanasi* became a green canvas ghost town. The countryside suddenly became quiet, and the work whistle stopped issuing its sonorous bleat. A few men could occasionally be seen wandering along the trails, but soon they too would be forced to evacuate to Delhi.

Mark had stayed back. He would have gone to Delhi with the others to await flight tickets, which Pendleton & Waxler was supposed to book, but he quickly decided against it. There couldn't be any harm remaining on a few more days, especially since he'd recovered most of his money. His mountain of bills could wait another week or two; it had already been six months.

Mark sat in the Samsara Club alone today. After what had just transpired, he decided to fall off the wagon with a bang. Udo Zreba, the owner of the tavern, stood quietly at one end of the bar. He looked like he'd been up all night, and his fingers worked tiredly through a box of crumpled receipts.

But the defunct business was only part of Udo's concern. Udo's sister had been missing for three days now, and everyone in their nearby village was becoming tacit and unusually reserved. Others were missing from surrounding villages, and concerning the rash of disappearances, everyone became eerily silent.

Mark spun around on the barstool. Dartboards, a pool table, and claw machines were being carried off, and someone came out of the back room hefting a spare cash register.

Mark swilled from a bottle of warm beer, and turned back to the disheveled businessman.

"It was one hell of a ride," began Mark, the trace of a slur in his voice. "It was really nice to know you, Udo, buddy!"

The dark-skin man nodded.

"Maybe they will try again in the near future. Perhaps whatever is the trouble will be quickly remedied. The very state of the international community depends upon it."

Mark nodded; but he wasn't listening.

He was thinking about Tatiana.

# 30
# Southern Maryland

Just before all hell broke loose, Douglas Rollins returned to his Southern Maryland home before continuing on to Washington. It would be a quick visit to the five-bedroom Greek Revival in Prince George's County; the presidential aide had an enormous workload mounting, and Tess wanted him back as quickly as possible. Among a growing list of other visitors Abraham Rosenblum, head of the Hades Project, was scheduled to arrive at the White House later that evening, following a detailed briefing at the Pentagon. The civilian arm's consultant had been given the highest civilian security clearances, and was privy to a plethora of national defense files concerning the Country's defense. It was no small assignment. Abraham been handed the responsibility of initiating America's new missile defense strategy, something President Brice had sanctioned, something that assured Tess that her global chessboard was properly arrayed, and Rosenblum's arrival was highly anticipated.

But when Douglas saw his son appear in the doorway of their home, national security vanished from his mind. And when his wife Pamela appeared, Douglas felt like the luckiest man in the world.

The family of three ate dinner, before gathering in the living room, beneath a large frieze of Napoleon at Waterloo. Douglas had purchased the curio at a Maine antique shop during the family's vacation three summers ago. Its bold strokes of oil depicted the battle-weary emperor riding his fiery steed into final battle.

Beneath the portrait stood Aaron, wearing his Citadel dress blues, the astute young cadet with a fiery gleam in his eye. Douglas adored his son, and felt an added chime of pride when he noticed the boy was wearing his *yarmelke.*

Douglas was Catholic, and his wife Sarah was Jewish. And when they first discussed the possibility of children it was established that their forthcoming progeny, no matter the gender, should share in the gifts of both traditional religions. Douglas loved the idea and became convinced Aaron would one day become a great leader of men, a true pillar of society.

The White House official would see to that personally.

Although Douglas would not be here long today, he always had time for a game of chess.

"Come here, young King David!" chortled the White House aide, extending his arms and embracing his only son.

He like to call him King David, and Aaron liked hearing it. Both men loved the victory of David over Goliath and, as far as Douglas was concerned, the circumstances surrounding the Philistine defeat was something every God-fearing person should remember.

Douglas then raised his glass of orange juice in a mock toast: "With my slingshot I will slay thee!"

"And with the Lord I will rule thee!" chimed in Aaron.

Douglas smiled. The boy was already charismatic and confident, ambitious and faithful in these formative years. And he was learning the art of diplomacy and discipline.

*Perhaps my very own son will one day emerge as President himself,* thought Douglas mirthfully. *Then I will have been part of two vanguard administrations. My boy is certainly compiling a strong foundation for his resume. Perhaps I should give him a full tour of the White House, just to make that dream seem even more attainable.*

"I issue a challenge!" cajoled Douglas, loosening the knot on his silk necktie.

"I accept!" exclaimed young Aaron, moving toward the piano. Atop the polished Baby Grand were the marble figurines of a chess set.

"What makes up the great general?" asked Douglas loudly.

"A combination of charisma, character and chess!" recited the boy, returning the couch and setting up the pieces.

"Do not forget about diplomacy!" chortled Douglas, snatching up his king. "Everyone must be heard, from both sides of the table! Remember what happened to Netanyahu!"

# 31
# Varanasi, India

When Mark finally caught up with Tatiana he was in no condition to pack. And neither was she, but that's exactly what Tatiana was doing. The front of her trailer was littered with stacks of boxes, file cabinets, and more tools than he could ever hope to count.

He'd come here to tell her the incredible news. Surely she would be dying to see the immense bone yard they discovered on Grid 41. But as he approached her tent he could hear the anthropologist arguing into her cellular phone. Then her line must have gone dead.

*"Hello? Hello?"* Tatiana pleaded. *"Artonus? Hello? Hello? Damn junk!"*

She then hurled the phone into the wild *Berrera* and kicked at the dirt.

"Are you okay?" asked Mark, walking slowly over.

"I am fine," replied the woman dejectedly.

"What's wrong?" asked Mark, slipping a warm bottle of beer from his pocket.

"My project funding is being stopped," she croaked. "They will not even pay for my flight back to Kiev."

Tatiana plopped down in the dirt and began to explain, through choking sobs, that she had been ordered to abort any and all research in and around the Indus Valley.

She wore the scowl of a jilted lover.

"I will have to throw everything away, and I am so close."

Mark popped the cap off the bottle, flicking it into the vines. He was glad he'd gotten his money back from Junior. "That really sucks, Tatiana. Where will you go?"

The anthropologist shrugged dejectedly. "I don't even know how I will ever be able to move everything! Ahmel has already left for Delhi, and I will only be able to make one trip. They are closing the entire area."

Mark nodded and took a swallow of warm Bud. Tatiana looked terrible. He could tell the anthropologist had lost weight since that first night at Grid 16, and Mark noticed dark circles forming under her eyes. She looked wound tight, and Mark wanted to go to her and begin rubbing her shoulders. But something was holding him back. For some reason it seemed important that *she* approach *him*, otherwise this intriguing woman might think he was only prowling for a piece of ass.

*I'd be running alongside Junior if that was the case,* he thought with the trace of a smile. *Before his little accident, that is.*

No, concerning Tatiana it was more than his libido, and Mark didn't want her to think otherwise.

"I'll help you," he said, stumbling into the rear of her Jeep. "I'm all yours today."

"Oh, Mark," whispered Tatiana, her voice laced with sadness.

As she went to his side Mark slipped his arms around her taut waist. Tatiana sighed and pretended to resist. "Mark, you are such a bad…"

But she never finished the sentence. There was the sudden rustle of vines, the snap and crackle of breaking branches. Tatiana's body went completely rigid. Mark hadn't heard a thing, and continued groping at the anthropologist affectionately.

Tatiana was clutching his shirt now, her eyes wide with fright. The swishing sound grew louder and Mark suddenly stopped pawing, turning his head toward the disturbance.

Then the *Berrera* seemed to come alive.

A military Humvee suddenly crashed through the vines like a bull elephant, foliage and weeds hanging from its front grill and an eight-foot radio antennae whipping from its hood.

"You folks have to get a move on!" barked the driver, wheeling toward the couple. "This is now a restricted area! Get whatever you need and get on the Delhi Road!"

"We're packing now," said Tatiana, releasing Mark.

The vehicle was about to pull away when the uniformed officer began glancing at a photograph taped to his dashboard; he then looked up suspiciously at Mark. "Is your name Black?"

Mark straightened up his posture, trying to look sober.

"Maybe."

"Get in," said the man; a second officer climbed from the Humvee and opened the rear door. "Someone back at the village wants to have a chat with you."

It was not a request, and Mark dropped the beer like a teenager who'd just been busted drinking by his parents.

"About what?"

"Get in and you'll find out."

Mark began drifting toward Tatiana, his hand reaching for hers.

"I'll be back as soon as I can," he said as his lips swept gently across her cheek.

Mark then stumbled reluctantly to the military vehicle and climbed inside.

As they drove toward *Green Village*, Mark began to feel a swelling knot of apprehension, and it seemed like every drop of alcohol began seeping from his pores. Junior had died. That had to be it. Or maybe he'd identified Mark as one of the vicious vigilantes.

Mark suddenly regretted having stayed back in *Varanasi*. He should have gone straight to Delhi with the others when he had the chance.

*What in the fuck was I thinking?!* thought Mark, seeing himself in an Indian court of law for attempted murder, maybe worse!

*But I only held the bastard down. I'll deny everything. They won't be able to prove a thing!*

Moments later they rolled into *Green Village,* and Mark immediately noticed a blue sedan parked beside Tent Number 4. He also noticed the radio aerial.

It *was* the cops.

"Mark Black, I presume?" asked a tall American as Mark stepped inside the tent.

*Maybe I shouldn't say a word,* thought Mark apprehensively. *I should ask for a lawyer, and not say anything that could incriminate me. They probably don't have many witnesses, maybe the Ratliff kid, but he's not too bright.*

At that moment Mark felt completely sober, scared straight, and was convinced that he could pass even the most stringent sobriety test. And from this point forward he would be very careful of what he said.

"I'm Agent Joe Richards of the FBI. I'd like to ask you a few questions."

Mark plucked a loose cigarette from his wrinkled shirt, and searched in vain for a match. "I'm listening."

"I'd like you to tell me what happened up on Grid 16. And start from the moment you struck it with your dozer."

"*It?*" thought Mark, surprised. *He is talking about That Thing in the field brush! This has nothing to do with Junior!*

Mark could feel his tension drop away, could feel the adrenalin running off. He took a seat on the edge of his bunk.

*Wheeeeew!* he thought with a surge of relief.

*I need a beer!*

# 32

Mark was numb with relief, as if he'd just received a last-minute stay of execution, a reprieve, full clemency, and couldn't wait to get back to Tatiana. The cops had scared the crap out of him, but after a few questions about the strange "hump" in the field, he was back out the door again.

But when Mark began hiking back to the trailer he didn't know whether he should continue to help Tatiana pack, or start thinking about packing his own things.

And as Mark trudged through the thick brush, he also began to feel a chord of sadness. This would be the end. Much as the multi-national operation had suddenly ceased, so too had this brief relationship. Tatiana would load up her artifacts and then disappear down the Delhi Road, if she hadn't already, and Mark wondered if he should try to accompany her back to the Indian capitol. He could be her escort, buying them some more valuable time together.

*And that would only postpone the inevitable*, he thought sadly. *Does she even expect me to show up?*

But a few of his many questions were answered moments later, when he lumbered up to her trailer and knocked. It was a memorable reception, to say the least. Tatiana flung open the door and snatched him up into her arms.

"I was wondering and worrying about you, Mark Black!"

She then yanked him inside the trailer, and slammed the door shut. Tatiana and Mark tumbled recklessly to the floor of the Ranchero, an impassioned tangle of arms and legs.

"But there is more," began Tatiana, running a brush through her hair before standing. Mark was shirtless and reclining on a throw pillow. He was studying the sexy woman as she pranced lightly around the room in nothing but her panties.

"And I simply cannot leave it behind," continued the scholar, going to the desk and grabbing her shorts. "And it is more than a thesis or dissertation, I can assure you."

Mark sprang to his feet and sauntered toward her. As Tatiana bent over to slip a long leg into the khakis, Mark reached from behind her and began fondling her generous breasts. He adored her florid and tender nipples, and he immediately felt an erection returning.

Tatiana turned to her American lover and reached for his swelling member.

"I have another place," she began softly, her eyes boring into his. "Where I am keeping some artifacts. They are safer there. Will you go with me?"

Mark was suddenly as hard as a slab of field granite.

"Do you even have to ask?"

# 33

Mark didn't know she meant right that minute.

But seconds later they were driving erratically along the piedmont of the mountain, a trail of dust whipping up behind them. As Mark found out, Tatiana wasn't fond of seatbelts, and that was another paradox. Her Jeep rattled and crashed down another trail, before disappearing behind a copse of *Berrera*. They wheezed through an arbor of vines, before rolling down a steep embankment, plowing recklessly onto the floor of the jungle. Mark was holding the overhead roll-bar like a monkey in a cage, and completely understood why the vehicle was in its current condition.

The forested floor was dark and cool, and as the ground leveled off it seemed as if they'd entered a cave. Tatiana navigated the Jeep across the muddy culverts made by earlier trips through here, and Mark began to see the front end of a camper sticking out through a thicket of gnarled growth up ahead.

"This is *Office Number 2*," said Tatiana cheerily, wheeling over a rotten limb and pulling up. "I keep many of my secondary supplies here. As well as some very interesting artifacts."

He could only imagine what 'interesting artifacts' stipulated, especially when Ahmel suddenly stepped from behind a tree.

The Egyptian exchange student was hefting an AK-47, and his face had a distant, vacuous expression.

"Ahmel!" said Tatiana surprised. "I thought you returned to Delhi?"

"I did," said the student flatly. He was looking around nervously at the walls of *Berrera*. "But I was told to return for you."

Tatiana rolled her eyes. "Let me guess! Artonus sent you?"

Ahmel nodded.

"Ha!" burst Tatiana. "Artonus will not even send me money to cover my expenses, and now he expects me to drop everything and come running to his protective arms! You tell Artonus…"

"He was rather firm, Ms. Borosky," interrupted Ahmel. "I think it would be wise if you returned with me. It is becoming dangerous here."

Tatiana was fumbling with a key chain. "That is impossible!"

"He says you must!"

Tatiana turned, and her eyes became angry slits. "Ahmel, listen to me very carefully! You can tell Artonus to kiss my *pushka!*"

Mark smiled at visions of doing just that, but kept an eye on the pushy foreign student.

Tatiana turned abruptly from her former assistant and went to the small camper. "Artonus does not own me! I left my chains back in the Ukraine!"

The anthropologist popped a padlock and flipped open a rusty flange. Ahmel remained behind her, returning his nervous gaze to the jungle, as if he could sense something. His brown eyes darted frantically through the *Berrera,* as if expecting a black rhino to burst through the foliage at any second.

Mark walked past the troubled student and stepped to the trailer, wondering what could be in there that was so important to Tatiana.

And when he turned back to Ahmel, the student was gone.

"Come in, Mark" he heard her saying.

Mark poked his head inside the camper. The leaky little compartment was cramped and cluttered, packed all the way to the ceiling with junk. The bulk of it was rolls of tent canvas, and he noticed two back-up generators and theJeep's spare tire amongst the clutter.

Tatiana was practically swallowed up amidst the shadows, but when her head popped from behind a tarpaulin he could see her eyes wide with excitement.

"Do you want to see a full skeletal assembly?" beamed Tatiana. "I have one in the back. I have nearly completed a second. I had been missing the cranium until now. Thanks to you, I have a complete assembly!"

Mark stuffed his hands into his pockets. "Sure, why not?"

Tatiana was standing before the sheet of plywood like a magician preparing to work her greatest magical illusion. "The Dravidians had written of them as well, and they called them the *brota!*" she began dramatically. "And I am convinced that you and I possess the only known specimens!"

Without further delay she turned and pushed aside the flimsy covering.

Mark felt a shockwave wash across him like a blast of air. The hulking figure standing before him reminded Mark of Tatiana's hunk of clay back at *Office Number 1*.

Tatiana was studying Mark, looking for a reaction. The dozer operator tried to remain calm and forced a smile. "Just what are those horns for?"

"They're not horns," intoned the anthropologist. "They are eyes, mounted onto stalks, like the decapods we all know and love: lobster, crabs and shrimp. And although those claws are an *ecto* design, this creature possesses a torso and thorax of *endo* design."

Mark didn't know what she was talking about. But he didn't ask any questions. None of this could be real.

"I have devised a few theories concerning their eyes," continued Tatiana didactically. "But they are mere assumptions. Perhaps they are necessary wherever they are from. Perhaps they hide in the dirt or sand, with only their eyes exposed. The eyes, probably resembling a native delicacy, are mere bait. And when the prey draws close enough to investigate the possible meal, whammo!"

She clapped her hands together, and Mark jumped.

"They leap up from the sand like a buried bear trap, swinging those giant claws! They certainly appear to be very effective tools for hunting!"

Mark nodded. That was obvious. The arm bones were long, thick and barbed, and seemed to be connected to the shoulder by a thick, pendulous clavicle.

"Since they're accustomed to mining through rock," continued Tatiana excitedly. "Slashing through flesh and bone is child's play."

"What do mean by *mining*?" asked Mark, looking perplexed.

"Those caves in the tunnel?" replied Tatiana, leering back at the skeleton. "You are looking at one of the culprits."

Mark forced a smile. Judging from its skeletal design, it certainly was a candidate for culpability.

"And," continued Tatiana. "It's safe to assume they are capable of both bipedal and quadruped movement, depending on the circumstances!"

She then pointed to the incredibly thick cranium.

"But don't let the size of its head fool you! I have already studied the brain cavity and spinal column! I believe they have a very primitive nervous system, in comparison to ours."

Tatiana then touched the enormous black skull. It was frightfully large and menacing, bigger than the one he'd found. "The skull you found was an adolescent. This is an adult. And although appearing large, this organ-housing can only accommodate a 12 ounce brain, something comparable to the *homo-erectus* of human ancestry."

Mark couldn't speak.

"Which brings me to the most unusual conclusion of all," continued Tatiana, crossing her arms.

*Perhaps I should think about getting on the road to Delhi a little sooner than expected,* thought Mark cooly.

No, he wasn't afraid of being attacked by one of these creatures. That was the last of his worries. It was his new lover he was worried about. Tatiana, though well schooled and very intelligent, was formulating a farce, a grandiose vision based on scattered pieces of obscure evidence. Sure, there were some unusual occurrences surrounding the rail project, but to create such a bizarre scenario was outright ludicrous.

*Or crazy.*

"And just what is your grand theory, Tatiana?" asked Mark guardedly.

"They didn't design that spaceship," she began evenly. "They do not have the intellectual capability. They are workers. Perhaps slaves. Something else is behind all of this, Mark, something we have yet to meet."

*Workers or slaves. Something we have yet to meet…*

They were his last thoughts before dozing off.

By the time they'd made it back to Tatiana's *Ranchero* it was well after dark and the many creatures of the night were on the prowl. The lovers shared some tea, and Mark listened to Tatiana's lunar prognostications as they lay bundled on the floor together.

*They didn't build that ship. They are not capable.*

The dream came with haunting clarity and definition. Mark could see them now, the skeletons in Tatiana's reserve trailer, stalking through the *Berrera* vines, their eyes poking through the thickets in search of a meal. The ungodly lobsters had heads the size of basketballs, but shaped like a GE light bulb. Their eyes were black and shiny, mounted atop the stalks, with tiny folds of skin sliding down like tongues, lubricating the small oval orbs.

Tatiana was suddenly standing at his side.

"Do you think they're nervous?" he whispered.

Tatiana didn't respond. She was holding her AK-47 now, and watching them closely.

"Just where did they…?"

*"Sssshhhh!"* she implored. "And stop smiling! They'll see your teeth and

take it as a threat!"

The creatures began moving, awkward lopes, their enormous arms dragging in the dirt. Mark didn't see any ears and they each had a blunt, flat nose. Their mouths appeared small, but that was a deception. As the python unlocks its jaw, so did this creature, yawning like a great cat, several gnarled rows of pointed teeth fanning out.

"Raise your arms!" barked Tatiana, now suddenly without her gun. "We must look submissive."

Mark obliged, and the creature did the same, its three long fingers (and what resembled a thumb) dangling over its unusual head.

Mark then noticed that they had some kind of weird apparatus strapped to their backs, a small device with a coil attached.

Then he suddenly woke up.

# 34
# Grid 16

Milton Hickers was up at the crack of dawn.
And he was going to get to the bottom of this.
*Today!*
*This morning!*
The university's high-density laser arrived ahead of schedule, along with three men from the Cal-Tech Sciences Department. The three post-graduates took their travel bags to an abandoned tent and wasted little time getting over to the site. As one man began snapping photographs of the alloy, the other two began to assemble the hi-tech "tool."

The laser had been shipped in sections, and packed tightly in wooden crates with excelsior shavings and Styrofoam blocks.

"You said you already tried to blast it out?" asked the scientist holding the camera; he was stroking the large metallic fin in the morning dew.

"Repeatedly," replied Milton Hickers, raising a cup of coffee to his lips. Jungle mist swirled around him and the morning sun cast a dull hue through the surrounding trees. "We packed and detonated nearly 50 pounds of industrial dynamite. Didn't even scratch it."

The Cal Tech scientist with the camera began climbing onto the horn, clumsily straddling the hunk of synthetic material. "It feels like titanium, but it's probably more like a synthetic aluminum. I'm willing to bet it absorbs radiological energy and reflects heat, which is why you had no luck with blasting."

Milton looked on in amazement as the man continued. "I'm also willing to bet that it has the capability to stretch."

Milton turned to the president of the Cal Tech Sciences Department. The bearded man was silently assembling the various parts of the intriguing weapon, his hands working deftly.

"Just what do you think we're dealing with, Mr. Kloppermann?"

The scientist smiled conspiringly, glancing around at the growing crowd of onlookers. "Let's take a little walk over here, shall we Milton?"

Once they were at a distance from the others, Walter Klopperman leaned toward Milton, his tone hushed. "I'm not going to mince words, Mr. Hickers. I think we have a bona fide, authentic, genuine Unidentified Flying Object here! *A UFO!* This will be one to tell your grandkids about!"

# 35

"This is *Cyclops*," began Professor Klopperman, glancing proudly at the fully-assembled tool. "It's an *SDI* prototype that never made it off the launch pad."

Milton was gazing absently at the hi-tech instrument, hands stuffed inside his jacket pockets. The laser looked like a giant cylinder with a glass eye. "Didn't that have something to do with Ronald Reagan and *Star Wars?*"

"That is correct," replied Dr. Klopperman. "The Pentagon donated it to our university, and we upgraded it significantly. *Cyclops* can cut through any known element, organic or inorganic."

The light beam was invisible at first. But everyone knew it was there, as the snaps and pops of the alloy signaled intense friction. Soon the skin of the vessel began changing colors, from black to a gray, an ashen hue. Then a rancid smell began wafting through the air.

"Take it up to Level Seven, Marcus," instructed the professor to the bearded post-graduate.

The man turned the dial, and the beam of energy became visible, a vague thread of red effulgence. Seconds later the translucent ray began cutting into the skin of the craft, and smoke began pouring off the vessel's horn.

At least 50 men were standing around now, staring in awe and wonderment, every bit as fascinated by the laser as the ship it was cutting into.

"Take it up to Level Ten, Marcus!"

The professor's tone was firm.

The technician flipped the dial to its maximum strength, and the vague red beam turned dark purple. Smoke was billowing now, and the exposed skin of the ship began to warp.

"I think we've nearly got it!" cried Klopperman over the *hisssss* of cutting pressure. "Rotate the axis, and roll it around the entire circumference!"

The beam of light was steadily worked around the horn, prying away the top like a magical can-opener. After twenty-seven minutes the laser was turned off, and one of the scientists wearing thick rubber gloves clambered back onto the horn, which was slightly misshapen now. He removed the severed tip, and handed it down to a man standing beneath him.

Then his head disappeared inside the immense hull.

"What can you see, Harold?" called Professor Klopperman.

The man's head popped up seconds later. "I can't see a damn thing in there. I need some light."

But before someone could toss him a lantern, a Geiger counter began jumping erratically.

"Holy Christ!" burst Professor Klopperman. He was leering at the red needle as it leaped erratically before his eyes.

"That thing's as hot as Chernobyl! Everybody get back!"

# 36

The *Argus*, one of America's deep-space military satellites, was whisking around the earth at twelve-thousand miles an hour, obediently maintaining a programmed orbit as it moved around the indigo convex of the planet. The quiet blue curvature of the earth was peaceful and pacific, yet far below, across the Eurasian continent, banks of cirrus clouds could be seen churning, obscuring the satellite's visual and photographic capabilities.

But the *Argus* did much more than take pictures of the terrestrial landscape; it looked for radio-active signatures, those which would indicate the presence of plutonium or uranium stores. Terror elements were now being scrutinized with every arm of American Intelligence, including what the Pentagon termed certain 'technological advantages.'

As America walked proudly into the 21st Century, she remained vigilant, especially for unchecked nuclear materials. And it was fully understood by America's military establishment that, despite her enormous military might, the United States could do little in the face of a mushroom cloud along the east coast.

But nuclear weapons left distinct chemical traces. These radioactive signatures could be detected through the heaviest of cloud cover, and as the military satellite began sweeping south of the equator, whisking toward the subcontinent of India, its sensors began to sweep the surface with an invisible prism of lasers; and as the concentric fingers passed along the Himalayan Great Range, the troubling images were relayed to a USAF outpost in Anchorage, Alaska.

For years the unremarkable concrete building had gazed into the teeth of the Soviet Threat. If the Doomsday missiles were coming, they'd be coming across the Bering Strait. The quickest way to a target was a straight line, and since the Soviets were unable to successfully deploy tactical "nukes" anywhere in the Western Hemisphere, their strategic arm became quintessential to the unwritten policy of Mutual Assured Destruction. The threat had been very real.

And very menacing.

In just under twenty minutes the Soviets could send hundreds of Intercontinental Ballistic Missiles raining onto American cities.

But that threat was gone. And soon after the Soviet Russia's dissipation, the American outpost was converted to a worldwide surveillance and communications station.

And as a signals officer manning the reception console began receiving the signatures, he snatched up a secured telephone.

"Sir, we're getting unusually high levels of radiation from Western Asia!"

There was a pause on the other end of the line.

"Where in Western Asia, Lieutenant?"

"India!" blurted the young officer. "Near the Ganges River!"

In under a minute the colonel was in the signals room, gazing at the feedback rolling off an electric printer. The stencil arm was jumping wildly, revealing a pattern of jagged lines.

And only minutes after that, as a corresponding satellite began snapping pictures, the officers were gazing at a magnified image of the area near Mount Everest.

"Pakistani Terror?" asked the lieutenant.

"A pretty isolated region for Terror," intoned the colonel.

"Fuel rods?"

"It's likely," replied the colonel dryly.

Then after a moment of silence, he turned to his subordinate. "Get me the Pentagon."

# 37

President Contessa Brice was seated behind her desk in the Oval Office, her eyes combing across the austere figures seated around the room. All of her appointments had been cancelled, and at 12:05 p.m. Douglas Rollins began rerouting her entire schedule. Instead of meeting with Maryland Senator Barbara Mikulski to discuss a Federal shipbuilding contract at Bethlehem Steel, the Joint Chiefs of Staff were seated around her office, as well as the Secretary of Defense, Melvin Knoll, and the chief of the NSA, Adam Kensington.

Secretary Knoll was thumbing through a stack of satellite thermal images. The photos looked like a weather map, with a hazy red glow emanating from the base of Mount Everest.

"We think its spent fuel rods," began the Secretary of Defense assuredly. "But we've got some men on the way over now to get a firsthand look."

"Just what else could it be?" asked the NSA chief, shifting his gaze to the photographs spread across the President's desk.

"A leaky reactor," intoned a three star general in accompaniment. "Or an unstable warhead would produce a similar signature, neither of which seems a very likely scenario. India has no reactor anywhere near the Himalayas."

The President nodded. General Riggs would know. Riggs headed the U.S. Nuclear Proliferation Watch Team. The Pentagon not only knew where all of its own bombs were stored, but those of every nation possessing nuclear capabilities.

"Or warheads," added the general.

"It certainly sounds like fuel rods," surmised the President after a moment.

"Maybe they got caught with their pants down," added Secretary Knoll. "It wouldn't be the first time."

"It would certainly help to explain a lot," rejoined Kensington.

Contessa Brice listened to every word carefully. She knew it didn't make sense, but also knew there had to be an explanation, and that it was her job to find it. Something told her it was a case of spent fuel rods, but she couldn't understand India's denial of the material. They certainly couldn't have forgotten about such a dumpsite.

*And still no sign of casualties or large scale contamination. At least the leak seems to be well-contained.*

"We should have some concrete information in a few hours," rejoined Secretary Knoll. "The IAEA, as well as some of our own experts are en route. ETA in just about two hours."

President Brice then asked for specifics.

"From what we're being told," began Secretary Knoll. "A team from Pendleton & Waxler, a construction firm out of Montana, came across the large storage container."

Tess was well aware of the immense rail project, and had long ago bestowed the graces of the Executive Branch. If there was going to be world cooperation in the War on Terror, there needed to be world cooperation on other fronts, namely those involving business and finance.

"Okay," began Tess, turning to her Secretary of Defense. "All work being conducted by American civilians in the area is to cease immediately, at least until we get a firm grasp of the situation."

"Already taken care of," chimed Melvin Knoll. "Central Pacific Railroad has already distributed over two-thousand pink slips."

"Good," began the President, standing. "You know I don't like surprises, Melvin."

# 38

When Tatiana dropped off Mark on the outskirts of *Green Village,* to pack what few belongings he had, the people from Washington were already on the scene. An entourage of military personnel from India's Defense Ministry accompanied the American agents, and it began looking serious when Mark saw the small convoy of decontamination trucks and men in bio-hazard suits headed off to Grid 16 with truckloads of equipment. Others stalked slowly through *Green Village* with Geiger counters.

And then the giant net dropped.

Everyone and everything was suddenly subject to a thorough screening. Footlockers were flung open, and all heavy equipment and private vehicles were carefully checked for possible contamination. But, as the tents were cleared and the men checked, nothing out of the ordinary was discovered.

And that alone was considered highly unusual. Radiation levels in and around the mysterious vessel were astronomically high, Chernobyl high, cracked-reactor meltdown-high, and corresponding readings were being recorded from space as well, confirming what those on the ground already knew.

But Mark didn't care what they found. As long as they didn't hold him up too much longer. He and Tatiana were planning to leave for Delhi, and as he stuffed an armful of clothes into his duffel bag, he wondered about this man Tatiana called Artonus.

As Mark grabbed a bottle of cheap cologne, he heard a rapping on the plastic panel at the tent's entrance.

"Excuse me," began someone from Washington. "I'd like to ask you a few questions."

Two others came in also.

"Sorry for all the commotion. Do you have any identification?"

Mark produced his wallet, wondering if the assault had finally caught up with him. He handed over his Maryland driver's license and in mere minutes his name was circulating through the FBI's Interpol data, as well as the new *COLOR* worldwide data base.

*COLOR* was something put forth by the President herself when she was heading the National Security Agency. This new system overlapped with a number of other data bases around the globe, allowing authorities from the *Big Eight* to access volumes of data with a flick of the fingers. Everything of even marginal relevance was entered into the enormous file, including over one-billion individual fingerprint profiles.

After running his name the tight-lipped men explained the possibility of spent fuel rods, and then they abruptly departed.

But before leaving one of the men turned back to Mark and glanced at his watch.

"You and the others will be taken to Delhi in about an hour. We've got a bus on the way now. Enjoy your trip back to civilization."

"Thanks anyway," replied Mark, stuffing an armful of socks into his bag. "I've already got a ride. She should be here in a few minutes."

The agent stepped back inside the tent and turned slowly to Mark. "Who is this *she?*"

"A friend," replied the heavy equipment operator. "She stays in a trailer about a mile from here."

"I'm sorry, but that's not possible," began the agent evenly. "The bus is running late, but it should be here momentarily. You can call her from Delhi when you get there with the others."

Mark looked up, his eyes narrowing. "I said I'm leaving with Tatiana!"

The agent stepped closer. "You obviously didn't hear me. As of *right this minute* no one is permitted in or out of this complex. To try and leave will be in direct violation of an Executive Order. You don't want me to arrest you."

"I've already been tested!" shot Mark, tossing an armful of clothes toward his suitcase. "Nothing is wrong with me!"

"But your lady friend has not."

# 39

Delhi officials remained adamant that India was in no way responsible for the present radiation. Their intransigent position created strain between the foreign Embassy's, while doing little to explain what was happening.

But the Pentagon already knew that the radiation was not the result of spent fuel rods. And at the behest of India's *Lok Sabba*, the United States Marines took complete control of the situation. The Biological Containment Division roped off the area, restricting all civilian traffic within a 50-mile radius. But, thankfully, their Geiger counters continued to indicate radiological containment.

Along Grid 16 it looked as if they were filming a movie set on planet Mars. Everyone was wearing a biological 'space suit,' and tracts of powerful lights lit up the darkening landscape with stark efficiency. Men were walking all around the vessel now, taking air and soil samples, radiological readings, thermal images, while recording any and all visual observations.

"This thing should be as hot as Chernobyl," began one Marine into his helmet radio. "But it's a very clean burn. Like the rays of the sun. It's somehow been filtered."

"What is being used as a filter, McCraken?" came a voice into his radio headset.

"I don't know," said the Marine. "But as soon as the energy is released, its being burned, in the exact amount it is dispersed. It's the most efficient thing I've ever seen."

# 40

The handcuffs were too tight, his thumbs were getting numb, and Mark Black needed to scratch his nose.

And as the Bluebird bus rumbled out of *Green Village,* bouncing rudely along the rocky trail, Mark's face was jostled off the Plexi-glass window. At least thirty others had been herded up as well, but Mark was the only one wearing restraining devices.

There had been no getting around it, and Mark thought he might just start crying. The bus grumbled through the jungle, passing the overgrown trail leading to Tatiana's trailer. Just over the hill, sticking out of a bank of *Berrera* was the *Ranchero,* with Tatiana sitting alone in the coming darkness; and Mark felt like he was being shipped off to some gulag.

*I never even got to say goodbye. And with all this commotion I'll probably never see her again.*

As the bus wheeled down the Delhi Road, leaving the horn of Everest behind, Mark was sorry he never got the chance to tell her his true feelings, to tell Tatiana that she inspired him, that she instilled wonderment and a true sense of purpose and possibility.

Unable to hide his painful expression, Mark felt a tear running down his cheek.

"I want to see a fucking lawyer!" he howled at the top of his lungs. His feet then began kicking wildly at the seat in front of him: *"I-Want-A-Fucking-Lawyer!"*

"Pendleton & Waxler has done it again!" roared someone in the packed lobby. The Delhi Hilton was booked to capacity and a fresh flux of grumbling guests were gathering at the front desk. Tool boxes, duffle bags and suitcases were piled high near the elevators, and a line of taxis were waiting at the main entrance.

"And they're gonna regret it!" boomed another voice.

The crowd was growing unruly, and Mark couldn't stop thinking about Tatiana.

*Was she safe?*

*Has she made it out?*

*Was she in danger of being exposed to radiation?*

He'd already tried her cell phone numerous times, and got only her voice mail. He knew that even that was a long shot, and he was hoping she had the presence of mind to retrieve it from the brush.

*Where she'd heaved it!*

Mark already knew she wasn't in Delhi, either. At least not yet. He'd already checked all the surrounding hotels, even the tiny motels, and her name didn't appear on any registry. But that didn't really surprise him. Mark knew Tatiana would never surrender her research, her passion, because of some evacuation.

He knew she was still back there, in the Himalayan valley, probably huddled and frightened in a corner at *Office Number 2.*

*And alone.*

And there was absolutely nothing he could do about it.

Foreign camera crews began arriving at the hotel, and Mark thought he saw Ted Koppel milling through the hotel lobby, interviewing workers.

But the heavy equipment operator shrank from the throng of commotion and bright lights, returning alone to his shared room to nurse a bottle of whiskey. He knew he shouldn't be drinking, but he didn't care any more. He went to the window and stared into the dark sky.

But he wasn't alone very long. A driller from California stumbled into the room with a female companion; they collapsed onto the bed arm in arm.

"Marky-Mark! *Whaaaaas Up?*" blathered the man. "Since you didn't want to come to the party, we decided to bring the party to you!"

Mark didn't remember the man's name, but knew he was one of the men who'd beaten Junior into the hospital.

As the two people slithered and rolled across the sheets, Mark went to the bathroom and closed the door behind him. He took a seat on the toilet, and again began dialing Tatiana's cellular number, which he'd memorized. He listened to the inane ring but, to his joyous surprise, she suddenly answered.

Mark bolted to his feet.

"Tatiana, it's me, Mark!"

"Mark?" she shrieked, before her voice began tailing away. "Where are you? I have been waiting…"

But the static became steady and strong and he could barely hear her.

"They made me leave!" he cried into the phone. "They handcuffed me to the back of a bus and brought me here to Delhi! Are you all right?"

She didn't seam to hear him. "Some men are trying to…"

Again, static filled his ear, and seconds later he was listening to a dial tone. After trying repeatedly to call back, he decided that her battery was getting low.

*Probably dead.*

Mark returned quickly to the window and gazed into the darkness. He should have never left without her, should have never left her side.

"Hey, Marko!" called the man from the bed. "Come on and have some fun!"

Mark turned. A third person had entered the room, and was sitting between them, hefting a tall USA reefer bong. The pungent smell of hashish began wafting through the room, and Mark decided to take a few hits, reeling as the trenchant smoke filled his lungs.

The bong went round and round, and Mark's eyes became red and glassy. His brain seemed to be floating in formaldehyde and he continued to pretend to listen to their inane banter. But he couldn't have been further from his new acquaintances.

And Mark began feeling even more lonely. His heart began racing when he remembered that Tatiana was out there, somewhere, alone, and that even the government was beginning to panic. What was she trying to tell him before they lost the connection? Was she in trouble? Was she being sent to Delhi by the government people? She'd mentioned others, and Mark he knew needed to find her.

*And that's not going to happen if I sit here all night with these jokers!*

Mark returned to the lobby, moving through the mob that swamped the front desk. His eyes darted frantically across the many faces laying siege to the hotel manager, hoping Tatiana would miraculously appear, her bright eyes alive with excitement. But he saw nothing but grumbling construction workers and a team of television reporters setting up their equipment.

Mark felt suffocated in the mob and needed to get some air. He stepped outside, into the parking lot, his eyes combing through the rows of vehicles, looking for something he could easily "borrow." But there were too many witnesses around to hot wire something, and if he somehow got arrested he knew he'd lose his mind.

Mark stalked around behind the hotel, where it was quiet, and gazed into the star-flecked sky. He began to realize that Tatiana had probably been right about everything. Something very big was going on, something that warranted American intervention in a foreign country, something that meant immediate suspension of the planet's largest multi-nation agreement, something that resulted in a widespread evacuation.

*Something Big.*

Mark couldn't have felt more powerless. He tried to remember what his sponsor had said about serenity and acceptance, and he tried to remember the *Serenity Prayer*. But he couldn't. Amidst all this jumbled insanity, he'd managed to meet the most wonderful woman, someone in hot pursuit of the incredible, someone in pursuit of her dreams.

*And I happened to be the lucky recipient of her secrets and passions.*

The glimmer of the stars was like the gleam in her eyes. And then Mark realized it wasn't a star he was looking at. The bright glob of light had appeared overhead and began moving slowly across the inky canvas above.

"Excuse me!" someone called.

A bright light accompanied the voice.

"I'm Ernie Bower with *National Enquirer!* Can you tell us what you know?"

A large camera lens was in his face and the stars were quickly forgotten.

Mark tried to ignore the man, walking in the opposite direction. But the crew stayed with him.

"What can you tell us about the alien space ship? Were you part of the discovery?"

Someone had finally said it! Mark hadn't heard anyone but Tatiana refer to it as an alien ship. Maybe Milton, and Torelli and the others were indeed hiding something, something big.

*They had to be.*

*And that meant Tatiana had been right all along!*

Mark felt a new sense of regret for doubting her, for thinking she was the one in outer space.

Mark suddenly stopped. He turned back to the paparazzi reporter and smiled ominously. *"You want to know about the spaceship? You want to know what we found up there in Borabi? You want to know specifics? I'll do one better! I'm the one who found the thing, and I'm the one to take you there!"*

# 41

As the *National Enquirer* van crept slowly along the Delhi Road, back toward the hills of *Borabi,* three U.S. Marines were being lowered inside the alien vessel. The soldiers were wearing bright orange bio-suits, with hands-free radios attached to their headgear. The lights on their helmets resembled those belonging to the miners of yesteryear.

Radio contact was steadily maintained.

"It looks like a hibernation chamber," began one Marine, dangling by a rope in the immense hull. All around him was a sprawling honeycomb of cocoons.

"There are at least ten thousand individual cavities. Either they're all dead or they're sleeping."

A group of American *Intelligence* agents were gathered outside a tent at *Green Village.* "Can you clarify, *Gemini?* Over."

There was a pause, then: "It looks like some kind of hive," crackled the voice. "A giant honeycomb of cocoons."

"Do you see any tools or flight controls?" asked a field agent. "How about Electronics?"

There was another pause.

"Negative. Just the individual chambers in the nest. It must be driven by some form of nuclear propulsion. Very sophisticated."

"Can you get our labs a few specimens?"

A pause. Some static...

"I don't know. We may need a few hand tools. It looks like we'll have to cut them out."

# 42

The unborn creatures looked dreadfully deformed, with large heads nestled atop shriveled bodies. A Marine sank his knife through the plasma wall, and a translucent gel began spilling out. The unusual larva were stored in the ooze, with a network of red cords attached. It appeared that they were being housed in some form of suspended animation, something similar to cryogenic preservation.

As the other men began slashing deliberately through the fleshy walls, a fetid smell permeated their masks and the primordial ooze began spilling out rapidly. It was almost as if the chambers were bleeding.

"Just where in the fuck is the engine room and bridge?" shot one Marine, his hand covered in a noxious gel.

"I don't know," replied the company commander. "Let's get these critters and get the hell out of here. We'll worry about that later."

He didn't know if he was seeing things. The lead Marine thought he saw a set of tiny eyes moving, but continued cutting through the membrane, before reaching in for one of the small contorted bodies. Then a tiny arm began swimming in the translucent shell, flailing painfully.

As if someone had turned on a microwave oven, waves of radiation began bombarding the vault, and an unusual sound could be heard, a high pitched whir.

"I think we triggered an alarm, *Alpha*, over."

"All right, get out of there, *Gemini*," came the speedy reply from *Green Village*.

But before the Marine could respond, three bony fingers poked beneath his mask, and he could feel the radiation bombarding his body.

Before falling unconscious, his eyes darted to the large honeycomb of chambers.

All of them were moving now! Swimming frantically in the little globules of liquid.

Less than an hour later, three specimens were dropped into plastic bags and flown back to the States to be identified.

Washington was immediately notified.

# 43

When Mark finally made it back to *Varanasi* he was covered in red mud and *Berrera* thorns; and he wasn't dancing around Tatiana's trailer. The heavy equipment operator was hunched behind a gnarl of *Berrera*, his heart beating rapidly. He could see the moon through the overhead canopy of trees, and a symphony of crickets filled his head.

As Mark drew a deep breath, beams of light danced around him as the uniformed men continued their search. He could hear their radios crackling through the trees, but laid motionless and still in the vines.

"Come on out, buddy!" one of the soldiers had shouted.

The man walked right past him, his flashlight beam dancing across Mark's dark shirt. "You are in grave danger here!"

Mark ignored the harsh admonitions, and about an hour later, as the last flashlight beam disappeared up the trail, he got to his feet and continued his trek through the jungle.

*The* National Enquirer *never got their story,* thought Mark, jumping through a bank of vines.

*And that's too bad.*

Mark had left the tabloid people on the Delhi Road when the van was suddenly stopped by a military contingent. But instead of being turned back with the others, Mark sprang immediately from the sliding door and disappeared into the brush. The soldiers took chase, but Mark never looked back, crashing through the *Berrera* like an escaped felon. He remembered the last ride back to Delhi, and was determined not to repeat that mistake.

Although it was very dark, Mark knew he was heading in the right direction; he also knew he was getting close. Just moments after avoiding the soldiers, Mark stalked quietly past *Green Village*, looking down from the forested hills as the American agents milled about. He could see a bright glow of lights a few miles away, where Grid 16 was located.

Mark found Tatiana's Ranchero about an hour later and, as he'd long suspected, Tatiana wasn't there. There was no sign of her ramshackleJeep, either, and the trailer's lights were out. Mark didn't think he'd have much of a chance locating her second camper at night, but decided to give it a try anyway.

Before continuing his journey, Mark stepped inside the *Ranchero* in search of something to drink. He knew Tatiana kept a case of bottled water under the desk; but as he began sorting through boxes in the dark, he heard a sound behind him.

*"Psssssssssssss! Psssssssssssss!"*

He could suddenly see her silhouette in the back room of the Ranchero, and stepped cautiously toward the dark recess.

"Keep the lights out!" she whispered. "I have candles."

Seconds later a circle of light flickered between them.

"You should have stayed in Delhi," intoned Tatiana darkly. "I had no idea how dangerous it would become, Mark."

The heavy equipment operator looked around the dark room. "Well, I'm here now."

They sat on the desk, which Tatiana had cleared, and gazed into each other's eyes. Tatiana looked like a tour guide for a haunted house, and the rings under her eyes had darkened. Her hair was a tangled mess now, and her bloodshot eyes were wide with fear, occasionally darting around the room.

"They come from a place of darkness," began Tatiana in an eerie calm. "Their planet must have limited sunlight."

Mark only listened in silence.

"They communicate by using pheromones," she added darkly. "Like a colony of ants."

Mark thought he heard something and turned quickly to the window. "Why are they here?"

Tatiana shrugged. "Perhaps they destroyed their own planet."

Again, he heard the noise and turned.

Then he felt her lips brush against his cheek.

"Thank you for keeping Junior in his place back there," he heard her whisper. "I knew what you were doing, and I wanted to thank you."

"Junior is trouble," replied Mark, his gaze fixed on the window now.

"I wouldn't have gone anywhere with him."

Tatiana then stifled a nervous chuckle, and turned away. Mark inconspicuously studied her. He hoped Tatiana wasn't starting to freak out again.

A flashlight beam suddenly filled the Ranchero, and Mark dropped to the floor. The soldiers had found him, and Mark laid still and silent; but the beam was fixed upon him.

"Hey, you! Come on out here!"

Tatiana dashed to the door and flipped the lock. Together they vanished into the back room as the man began beating his flashlight against the trailer: "You folks are in danger! You must leave with me now!"

A helicopter suddenly roared overhead, its spotlight passing across the Ranchero.

Mark looked out the window and stared at the man near the door. He was wearing military khakis and an M-16 was slung across his shoulder.

But then he saw something else, something emerging from the banks of *Berrera*.

Then another one.

They began trouncing across the dirt in awkward lopes, little beasts, hideously deformed children at play. A scream pierced the night air, and chirps and whistles chimed aloud. The rifle erupted, bright muzzle flashes.

Tatiana blew out the candles.

Then they listened in silence as the soldier was torn to pieces, his body dragged off into the wooded tract.

In sections.

Through the window he could see another one sitting high in a tree, an owl from hell.

It was feeding time.


They hardly moved the rest of that night.

And Mark and Tatiana didn't sleep.

Not a wink.

And at first light they started to pack.

Furiously.

# 44
# The White House

"They just arrived at Fort Dicks, Maryland," began Secretary Knoll, replacing the portable telephone.

The President turned slowly from the scenic view and nodded. Contessa was standing on the Truman Balcony, overlooking the verdant hills of Virginia. She had already raised the Nation's security status from a peacetime *Defcon 5* to a *Defcon 3,* an added precaution in these sudden times of uncertainty. The President's cabinet was in full agreement, and her orders meant a lot. *Defcon* was a system the Executive Branch used to categorize a national threat, to anticipate and calculate the probability of conflict. Normal conditions of world peace placed the nation at a *Defcon 5.* But as trouble mounted, the scale would ascend in accordance to the perceived threat.

*Defcon-3 is measured and appropriate, she thought confidently.*

Her orders meant that the Joint Chiefs were on stand bye for large scale operations, and that the Fifth Fleet would be immediately deployed to the Indian Ocean.

Secretary Knoll was gazing down at a sheet of paper.

"But we've already learned a few things, nonetheless. They adults are larger than humans, and very hardy. They appear to be well developed physically, and have anatomies comparable to those found in mammals. They possess a four chamber heart, two lungs, and similar blood vessels and capillaries."

*At least they don't appear to be too different,* thought Tess.

But the Secretary of Defense seemed to read her thoughts.

"And that's where the similarities end," said Knoll.

"Abruptly," added Kensington.

"They possess both an outer skeletal design as well," rejoined Secretary Knoll, looking down at the report. "It's a melding of *ecto* and *endo* skeletal designs. A rather remarkable adaptation."

"How so?" asked Tess, looking on curiously.

Knoll flipped through the pages. "Their outer extremities, arms, legs and a portion of their skulls, are *ecto*-skeletal, like those of a decapods, and they have a rather formidable set of limbs. We think these creatures are ground dwellers, wherever they are from, and it appears they were recruited to mine something."

"And our boys also believe they have a rather unique hunting technique," began Kensington.

Tess knew they'd discovered several mass graves, and the onus of investigating the causes of the death was on the Indian Government. The President had even heard that one of the burial vaults contained over ten-thousand individual sets of bones.

"Pictures are on the way," added Knoll. "Along with some taped footage. We're installing cameras now. You'll soon be seeing live coverage."

"Are you familiar with the Komodo Dragon?" asked Adam Kensington; he looked like a teenage boy who'd just gotten hold of his first *Playboy* magazine.

Tess nodded. President Brice knew the Komodo Dragon was a large monitor lizard living on several islands in the south Pacific. Almost everyone knew that much.

"Well, their mouths are swimming with bacteria, and their bite delivers a cocktail of toxins, which renders its victims dead in hours. These creatures operate on a similar premise, with a much more effective toxin at their disposal."

When the President didn't respond, Kensington continued. "This is an assumption, but it's based on some swab samples."

"Keep studying that vessel," began Tess evenly. "Learn what you can. I don't think we can keep a lid on this. How are we going to let the cat out?"

"I don't know if it would be wise to say too much right now," intoned Adam Kensington. The *NSA* chief had moved to a chair near the French doors. "I think we should wait until we learn a little bit more. There's not much we can tell anyone right now. No sense in causing unnecessary alarm."

"I agree," replied Tess, turning to Knoll. "Do they pose a serious threat to us, Melvin?"

She knew it was a loaded question.

But Melvin usually ate those for lunch.

The secretary shrugged. "I don't think the United States is in much jeopardy. Not at this time, anyway. The ship has evidently been buried for some time, and we haven't had any overt problems until now."

"But now that they know they've been discovered, that could change things," began Kensington guardedly. "As long as they were hidden, they may have felt safe. But if they start feeling threatened, especially with us cutting up their ship, we don't know what they could be capable of."

"And those underground crypts are unquestionably a red flag," added President Brice, strolling to the front of her desk. "I don't know what to think. How could they stay alive for so long? I mean, are they multiplying?"

"Our boys think that ship is, amongst other things, a giant incubator of sorts. It contains multiple chambers with larva in various stages of development. One of the more mature creatures killed a Marine. So far, he's been the only casualty. We think a radiation signal triggers the growth process. The ship appears to be a time-released emergence chamber."

Kensington piped in, "It's pretty obvious that the vessel was designed for deep space travel, over incredibly extended periods of time."

"It almost looks like they may have been planning to colonize," added Knoll. "But, as we've mentioned earlier, we don't think Earth was their original destination. It's relatively safe to assume that they never intended to come here."

Tess waited for an explanation, and Knoll gave it.

"I think they were streaking through the galaxy and may have experienced some type of engine trouble. They saw that Earth was marginally conducive to their survival, and crash landed."

"And for reasons unknown," began Kensington. "But those probably involving great distances, they were never rescued."

"And it's also safe to assume that they didn't built that ship," surmised Knoll. "They are probably mere pawns in all of this, probably slaves or even prisoners of a higher life form."

Tess looked bewildered as Knoll continued. "And it looks like they were sent into space to mine something. That would be one explanation for the labyrinth of mines they discovered in that railroad tunnel. They were mine shafts."

"What could they be mining?" asked Tess, lowering her head.

"Whatever they need to survive. It could be anything from nitrogen-rich phosphorus, to sulfur oxide, or some other mineral. It may be required for their unique form of hibernation, or procreation. It seems that they emerge like the saketa, on a natural timetable."

Kensington nodded. "And they could be from almost anywhere. But I'm willing to bet they're from a nearby star system, possibly Tau Seti or Alpha Centauri."

President Brice glanced back at the morbid pictures taken from the mass grave. "At least we know what they did for food. I want a significant naval contingent present in nearby waters."

"Fifth Fleet has already been dispatched," replied Secretary Knoll. "They are being rerouted from a routine patrol through the Mediterranean. They're headed back through the Suez and should be off Ceylon within a matter of days."

"Tell them to step it up," intoned the President. "Until we know exactly what we're dealing with, I want our shields up."

Her eyes then flashed around the room. "Gentlemen, I can't imagine how we can expect to keep a lid on this. But until we know exactly what we're dealing with, keep to the center. Let the foreign agencies have their headlines, but until we have a firm understanding of the situation we'll treat this as a radiological hazard, and nothing more."

# 45

President Brice did not have to wait long for more information to arrive from Fort Dicks. The military scientists in Maryland were eager and thorough...

...and thoroughly amazed.

"It appears that their sun is much larger than ours," began Herbert Donnely, one of those men. Donnely, temporarily attached to Homeland Security, was wearing a plain blue suit and ill-matching yellow tie. President Brice studied the scientist from her desk in the Oval Office.

"This would mean a wider orbit, and longer periods of darkness," continued Donnely. "It's also possible that their planet is located much further from their sun, which is probably a few billion years older than our own."

"Do we have any idea of just where that might be?" asked Secretary Knoll. But the scientist continued addressing the President. "It's safe to assume that it comes from our galaxy, but the Milky Way alone contains over half a billion star systems."

"Probably somewhere nearby," surmised Knoll. The defense guru was seated near the window, gazing across the West Lawn of the White House. "Probably within the Orion Arm of the galaxy, and not too terribly far from our solar system."

President Brice glanced back down at the photographs spread across her desk. They were the shots taken of the mass grave discovered twenty miles north of the alien ship, and they told her enough to warrant the deepest concern.

"I want to contact Whitehall and the Kremlin," began Contessa, turning to Secretary of State Crofton. "I want all channels open."

The Secretary nodded. "Both Embassies have already stated that they've got small contingents of agents en route to the scene."

Secretary Crofton went on to explain that at least a dozen countries throughout Europe and Asia had teams en route, and that the list would probably double overnight.

House Speaker Harold Philbin was seated quietly in a corner of the office, looking much the outsider.

"I don't think we want to overreact," began the liberal power-broker.

Philbin was cheeky and round, built very much like a pork barrel, someone who reminded Tess of Benjamin Franklin and Ted Kennedy combined.

"And until we learn to speak their language, we'll never learn anything about their origins," continued the House Speaker. "I think one of the things we need to worry about is just how they communicate? You mentioned something about an unusual chirping sound. Is that their way of speaking?"

The scientist turned. "That's a very good question. We don't think they communicate with their mouths. They seem to reserve that exclusively for eating and breathing. The chirp you mentioned is, we believe, an evolutionary residual, something they'd eventually disregarded, but something that persists, nonetheless. As we have evolved from needing our appendix, they have turned their backs on language."

President Brice approached the scientist. "Do they use some form of mental telepathy?"

"Pheromones," replied the scientist assuredly. "It would explain their disproportionately large heads. They are equipped with pheromone receptors."

"The eyes are falling to the wayside as well," continued Donnley, walking across the office as if it were a stage. "Their heads are the recipient of most of the oxygen, which somehow feeds the dual skeletal design. It almost appears that their planet incurred a cataclysm of sorts, which rendered many of their original body forms useless, thus facilitating the drastic necessity for change."

The scientist's eyes then drifted to the desktop. "And these magnificent creatures found a way to make the changes necessary to survive."

"Do you think they have the ability to contact others?" asked Secretary Knoll, turning from the window and approaching. "The last thing we need is an alien death star rolling into our solar system."

Knoll's tone carried humor, but no one was smiling.

"They don't appear to have done so to this point," began House Speaker Philbin. "And if they haven't been rescued by now, they're probably out of earshot."

"Good," began the President, strolling back to her desk. Again, her eyes went to the Presidential Seal mounted to the wall. "Because I don't want them contacting anything right now. And I want some Special Forces sent over there, and tell the Fifth Fleet to run full throttle. We don't need this situation getting out of hand."

Now the House Speaker seemed to blush.

"Why are we taking a combative stance?" shot the congressman. "They will only perceive our actions as a threat! To this point they haven't raised a finger to hurt us! And now, less than two years after concluding a bloody war in Asia, this new administration seems bent on igniting another conflict, this one well beyond global proportions!"

"We lost two United States Marines!" shot the Secretary of Defense. "And that alone is a call to action!"

"That shit worked with Saddam and General Peng!" retorted the congressman hotly. "But these visitors are a little different, in case you haven't noticed!"

"So we're supposed to carry on, business as usual?" grumbled Kensington.

"Oh, I know what's going on here," began the congressman conspiringly; he was holding a finger up in the air, like Charlie Chan about to announce the name of the murderer.

"Would all this have a little something to do with some budget appropriations to help the Hades Project along? A little something to get us galloping right back into war?"

"It's not considered pre-emptive when something unknown enters our airspace!" roared Secretary Knoll.

"It's not in *Our* airspace!" shot Philbin. "It's not even parked in *Our* country!"

"*Our* is meant to include human civilization as a whole!" retorted Secretary Knoll, now standing nose to nose with Philbin. "And it must remain *Our* moral responsibility as the only remaining superpower to protect the planet as a whole!"

The liberal congressman seemed to boil over. "When you stop your corporate thugs from dumping toxic chemicals into *Our* lakes and streams, then we'll start talking about protecting the planet!"

"Stop this nonsense!" flared President Brice, her arm dropping like an arm-bar at a military checkpoint. The room fell immediately silent. "I won't have this partisan play in my office! Not at this time!"

"But you're planning to destroy something you know nothing about!" rejoined Congressman Philbin.

The President ignored the remark and turned to Secretary Knoll.

"Get the *Rangers* over there, Melvin," she began evenly. "I want to assure that our overseas citizens remain well protected."

Again, the congressman blathered in protest, but the President's position was firm.

Tess was only marginally interested in the remaining discussions. And as the congressman stormed out, promising to resume the battle from the Hill, Tess tried to absorb the mounting heap of abstract information.

And try to attach some kind of meaning.

She could not shake a gnawing sense of trepidation. Perhaps it was merely the fact that they were foreign to the Human Race, or maybe it was their frightful appearance that unsettled her. But whatever the case, they were gorging on human flesh as a means of survival.

They reminded her of an evil she'd once read about in the Bible.

# 46

When they reached Delhi, shortly after five o'clock in the morning, Tatiana took care of everything. And she worked with amazing speed and efficiency. After a lengthy visit to a man named Artonus, who was inordinately eager to help, Tatiana and Mark were not only booked two tickets on a freight-express airline, but a truckload of men appeared to help them transport all of her research.

And at ten o'clock that evening, as another planeload of reporters touched down in the Indian Capital, Mark and Tatiana caught the very last flight out of India.

And as their aging Boeing reached for altitude in the night sky, a set of electronic eyes fell upon them.

# 47

The nuclear-powered aircraft carrier *U.S.S. Harry S. Truman* crashed through the stormy Indian Ocean at 27 knots, its enormous bow undulating heavily through the rolling swells. As a thirty foot wave lopped over the tall freeboard, crashing down across the ship's forward deck, a wall of mist whipped into the towering island superstructure.

The forecast was calling for a break in the weather two-hundred miles to the southwest, and the American carrier continued running full steam toward the coast of India, where she was ordered to conduct reconnaissance sorties until the crisis passed.

The *Truman* carried a compliment of seventy aircraft, each possessing the most sophisticated technology and weapons in the world. The carrier's rain-slickened decks were clear now, but her runway lights remaining aglow, strings of blue dots bobbing along the sea of gray. Only two aircraft were out at sea, a pair of *Sea King* helicopters on routine submarine patrol. Until the weather broke, Admiral Donald Morrison wanted to keep his fighter wing in the safety of the hangars below.

Each *Sea King* was 100 miles out at sea, one off the port beam, the second off to starboard. Using sonar sensors lowered by cables, the choppers hovered for hours in stationary positions as their sensitive listening devices did their job. An enemy submarine was the *Truman's* biggest threat.

Until now.

The windows of the *Sea King* were doused with windy sheets of rainfall, reducing visibility to under twenty feet; but a lighted instrument panel provided electronic eyes, feeding altitude, fuel and wind-velocity readings.

As the chopper rocked in the wind a sonar officer, seated in the belly of the *Sea King*, was studying a glowing feedback monitor. Several feet away were the reinforced sonar cables, which ultimately led to the stormy waves below.

And beneath them.

Suddenly, the young Annapolis graduate began to squeeze his eyes shut. And then he opened them. It was still there, the large blinking dot on the screen.

"This is *King One!, Control!"* he began into his radio. "I'm getting an unusual signal! Vessel is submerged directly beneath us! Are you guys getting any of this, over?"

"We don't have it *King One*," came the speedy reply from the *Truman*. "Send us your position and read-out, over."

"They are not conventional screws! I'm getting a really bizarre signal. A whisper!" implored the *Sea King* signal's officer, flipping a radio switch and sending the electronic images across the ether. "It can't be a Russian boomer! They can't have anything that big!"

"We're confirming now, *King One.*"

"Getting what?" spluttered the admiral, turning to his weapons officer. The bridge of the *Truman* was a sprawl of heightened activity, and Admiral Morrison looked as if he was just ordered to clean the ship's latrines.

"Active sonar says it's nearly two-hundred meters long," continued the junior officer, shaking his head. "That's almost a quarter mile."

"Bring us around, right full rudder!" barked Morrison.

"Aye, Admiral, Right full rudder."

"*King One,* keep shadowing," began the admiral into a radio. "We're going to send our Russkie buddies a little message."

"He says he doesn't think it's a boomer," commented the ship's bridge officer.

"It's got to be!" barked Admiral Morrison. "What in the hell else could it be?!"

Then the helicopter sent another message.

"*King One* to *Control!* This fucking thing just rose out of the water! No visible flight decks, portals, radio antennae or even a propulsion systems! It's just hovering above the waves!"

Admiral Morrison was literally speechless. His eyes went to the bridge officer, and then swept across the bridge, stopping at every man. The captain approached.

"We should attempt to get some pictures."

"I have a better idea," muttered the admiral, approaching the radio. "*King One,* hold your position! Help is on the way!"

As the deck heaved, twin tongues of fire blew across the blast wall, and an explosion of steam sent the catapult racing forward. Seconds later an F-14 Tomcat was hurled from the *Truman's* steel deck like a giant albatross. As the warplane reached for altitude, a second *Tomcat* shrieked into the misty expanse, quickly bolting into a vertical climb at Mach-2.

Lieutenant Harold Lansing, affectionately called *Mongoose,* flipped on his *Heads-Up* Display and began scanning the gray expanse.

He noticed that an A-6 Intruder had joined the hunt, keeping low on the waves below.

And Lansing suddenly had *The Thing* on his display.

"*Goose,* this is *Control,* do you copy?"

"This is *Mongoose,* " replied Lansing into a throat microphone. "I copy, over."

"Get as close as you can, and keep the footage running."

"10-4, *Control.* "

Lansing was nestled in the cockpit as if sitting in an undersized recliner. A lighted instrument panel surrounded him, walls of glowing buttons and labeled switches. The wing man suddenly appeared off his right flank, the big Tomcat moving close to form a two-plane phalanx. Lansing could see his wing man's mask and helmet through the canopy; then he saw the pilot flip a thumb's up, followed by a quick salute.

"Let's run it up to thirty-thousand feet," replied Lansing, returning the salute. He then flipped an arming device on his weapon's console.

"And then we'll begin a gradual descent. I want to stay above the cloudbank as long as possible. It may work to our advantage."

"10-4, *Mongoose.* "

The fighters went to after-burner and screamed high into the stormy sky.

The order to open fire, to pre-empt a strike, was never formally issued. The training manual at the Annapolis Naval Academy stated that, in times of peace, fighter pilots were permitted to engage only if fired upon.

But the circumstances surrounding the incident, those gray areas of individual judgment, were as murky as the sky.

"It suddenly dropped off our monitors!" began *Goose* into his throat microphone. "But *Sea King One* places it at 22-degrees Longitude, 90-degrees Latitude."

Whatever it was, it was gone now.

Captain Lansing continued to monitor the discussion between the chopper and the *Truman,* unclear as to his next course of action. Perhaps their surveillance equipment was malfunctioning, or they were picking up a natural weather phenomenon.

"*Control*, this is *Mongoose*, should we bring it home? Over."

"Hold it!" crackled the voice of the *Sea King* pilot. "*Control,* we're getting another signal! Bearings 20-degrees Longitude, 89-degrees Latitude, and moving northwest. It's turning, *Control! This thing is enormous!*"

"Can you be a little more clear, *King Two,* Over?"

"I think it just saw us, *Control!*" spluttered the chopper pilot. "It's turning toward us, and it's coming our way! I see lights! *I think it just fired on us!*"

Then the signal was lost, and waves of static were filling Lansing's helmet.

That was all *Goose* needed to hear.

Even at fifty miles from the target, and obscured by fog and rain, the Tomcat's Phoenix missiles were well within striking range. And *Goose* didn't hesitate. Without clearance from the *Truman, Goose* squeezed a red firing button and a fat missile dropped from a wing mount, its own solid-fuel rocket igniting.

Having a mind of its own, the Phoenix streaked off toward the coordinates at Mach 5, impervious to the rain as it disappeared inside the clouds.

It was to become the very last battle sortie executed by the *USS Harry S. Truman.*

Admiral Morrison continued staring into the luminescent glow of a sweeping radar screen. The Tomcats were represented as tiny white dots, as were two Phoenix missiles streaking across the screen, tiny points of light blinking on the monitor.

"This is *King One*, Control! Do you copy, over?"

It was the missing chopper, and the *Truman's* bridge erupted in cheer.

"We're glad you're still with us, *King Two!* What's your status?"

"Our electronics are shot, *Control,*" came the voice through a wave of static. "We'll need some help getting home, over."

"10-4, *King Two,*" grumbled the admiral. "We'll send out a beacon signal, over."

"Do you think that's wise, Admiral?" intoned the ship's captain, a look of consternation draping his face. "It might reveal our position to the enemy."

"We don't have any enemies, yet, Captain!" shot Admiral Morrison, his face turning red. "And I'm not about to let our boys drop into the drink. I've got four men stranded at sea. They're getting low on fuel. Just what is it you suggest I do?"

The captain did not respond, and began moving away.

"Besides," continued the admiral, more to himself: "Whatever it is, it's gone now."

"Let's hope so," said the bridge officer.

# 48

It hovered above the stormy waves like the crest of *Poseidon*, an enormous black sphere. It was twice as large as the *Truman*, yet silent and motionless, sitting quietly above the rolling waves like a hovercraft, powered by some highly-advanced propulsion system.

Sheets of rain slashed across its sleek hull, and a band of lights occasionally flashed across its long tapered body. To the crew of the *Sea King*, it appeared to be hiding in the storm, taking refuge in the tropical depression.

What the chopper crew didn't know was that it was reading *Truman's* robust beacon signal.

The Unidentified Flying Object never saw the approaching *Phoenix* missiles.

The first Phoenix streaked down in a vertical plunge, a tailfin jutting from the rear of the rocket, adjusting its course heading several degrees. A third-stage radar sensor was activated inside the missile, and the target appeared between electronic cross-hairs; an internal arming mechanism was activated.

It struck the enormous vessel along its topside, and a great ball of light swept across the alien dome.

The hovering vessel rocked and swayed, stormy winds whistling across a foreign appendage which suddenly appeared on its hull. As the gigantic vessel turned, buffeting on the turbulence, a second *Phoenix* came streaking through the rain, its exhaust spitting a fiery trail of solid fuel residue. The anti-aircraft missile struck the vessel in nearly the same spot as the first, and a cascade of blue sparks began spilling into the ocean.

Before vanishing beneath the waves, the vessel's hull began vibrating like a giant tuning fork. Like giant smoke rings, three hoops of colored energy pulsated from its hull.

Growing as they moved across the waves, the radioactive funnels began sweeping toward the *Truman.*

Men stationed in the bridge and along the flight deck saw them first, the rolling walls of energy coming straight from the northwest, billowing toward the *Truman* like towering tidal waves. The first wave knocked out the ship's electronics, sweeping across the carrier in a hot radioactive wind; the gamma rays blistered and burned the entire crew, as if they were being cooked alive in a giant microwave oven. The many sailors would only have a few miserable moments of life remaining, enough time to see the second wave approaching.

The second radioactive tsunami blew across the deck like a cyclone, flipping aircraft and sending the carrier heaving to port, its superstructure resembling the Leaning Tower of Pisa.

The lift wells jammed, and anything that wasn't welded to the deck was blown into the sea.

But it was the third wave which caused the most damage, in terms of radioactive disasters. The *Truman's* nuclear reactor was shattered, and although her warheads remained in tact, the immediate waters surrounding the warship began to boil rapidly from the radioactive heat; and her many tactical warheads were suddenly exposed.

The aircraft carrier heaved and rolled recklessly across the waves, like a huge piece of sizzling bacon drifting in a vat of grease. Her reactor was ablaze and a series of explosions began ripping through the *Truman,* engulfing her many decks and incinerating her crew of nearly six-thousand. In a matter of minutes the immense warship was reduced to a blackened floating shell, and the hottest waves of radiation continued to wash across her freeboard and flight deck.

The *USS Truman* was a floating disaster area.

# 49

"It went down somewhere in the Indian Ocean," began Secretary Knoll; he was standing before the President's desk, holding an emergency dispatch from the Pentagon's Chief of Naval Operations.

The heavy calico drapes were open and natural light spilled into the Oval Office, making the brown wall-to-wall carpet look like an altogether different color; beige, matching the hue of her eyes.

"But the *Truman* came under heavy attack," continued Secretary Knoll.

The President began gazing intently at her defense chief; and she could tell that his next words would not contain good news.

"What is the *Truman's* status, Secretary Knoll?"

"She was destroyed, President Brice," began Knoll, his voice filled with contrition. "And her entire crew went down with her."

The President dropped back into her seat. "Oh my God."

"At least it was an even exchange," commented Adam Kensington. "They think the *Truman* may have brought *It* down as well."

President Brice didn't stay seated long. The flat of her hand smacked the desktop and she bolted to her feet. Her eyes burned intently. "Is that intended to make me feel better, Adam?"

"No," lamented the NSA chief. "And I apologize for my stoicism, President Brice. I was just trying to shed some light on this terrible and unforeseen tragedy."

"Now I will have to sign over six-thousand letters to the loving families of those great men and women! And just what am I supposed to tell them, Adam? That we think we may have shot down the alien *UFO* that we think committed this atrocity?"

"We recovered the Tomcat pilots about an hour ago," commented Secretary Knoll. "Other than the chopper crews, they were the only ones that made it."

"Melvin, how do we know her reactor didn't simply go up?" asked the President hotly. "Or that one of her warheads didn't inadvertently detonate?"

Everyone in the room was familiar with battleship *USS Iowa* and its peacetime crew sabotage.

But even as she asked this, she knew the answer. The circumstances at hand were indeed different, terribly unique, utterly abstract, and Contessa knew it. This tragic event was painfully consistent with an evolving pattern of events. The radiation readings in India, followed by the bizarre discovery. No, this was not a coincidence. And at this point, she didn't need to see a smoking gun.

The *Truman* was all the evidence she needed.

"Those things have begun stirring like crazy in their cocoons," injected Adam Kensington. "It's almost as though they know something happened."

"Perhaps they think we've declared war?" began Secretary Knoll, removing his reading glasses. "And I strongly suggest we get on a war footing."

President Brice was in full agreement.

"Alert *Central Command*!" she began evenly. "And raise our status to *Defcon-1*. I'm going to treat this as an act of war."

In a matter of hours, at the urgent behest of her Administration, Contessa Brice left Washington to conduct the unusual debacle from an undisclosed location.

And she would be glad she did.

But the President's problems were only just beginning.

# 50

The White House was empty.

Almost.

Within minutes after receiving news of the *Truman* incident President Brice was evacuated by the Secret Service, whisked aboard Air Force One in the middle of the afternoon. With an extensive canopy of fighter cover the President's helicopter began leapfrogging across the nation as it headed to Omaha where a secret bunker would become her next office.

With an altogether different staff.

Vice-President Joe McCain had slipped out of Washington as well, flying to a secret compound outside Dallas, Texas. And as the Nation's top executives fled the Capital, many remaining in the District became circumspect as to their own safety. Just what exactly was going on?

After refueling outside Louisville, Kentucky, Air Force One again ascended into the cool sunny sky, continuing its westward trek.

Secretary Knoll was seated across from the Commander-In-Chief, a stack of folders spread atop his lap. An overhead reading light was on and Knoll's glasses were creating an occasional glare in her eyes. As the chopper buffeted on a sharp wind, Tess saw the blinking lights of an Apache gunship flying very close air support.

"We still don't know if the *Truman* ever brought it down," began the Secretary of Defense. "But every carrier in the United States Navy is now at sea, and Britain has sent out a significant naval contingent as well, six aircraft carriers being among their task force. We can't control the entire world, but our plan is to at least secure the Atlantic Ocean."

Secretary Knoll produced a list of fleet positioning and patrol charts.

"We haven't had any other sightings and feel the Tomcats may have proved to be an effective deterrent. Our Tommys and Hornets are running continuous reconnaissance sorties along both coasts."

Tess was gazing absently at her military chief. She began to feel a returning sense of security discussing the situation with Melvin. He was an integral part of the previous Administration, and had almost single handedly headed the war against North Korea, a brief yet fiery conflict with minimal American casualties.

As Air Force One buffeted lightly on another pocket of air, an F-15 Eagle streaked overhead, its twin turbines pushing the fighter past the sound barrier; a roll of clapping thunder ensued.

"We're convinced that we can learn a lot from this unusual spacecraft, President Brice. Units on the ground in *Varanasi* report that it possesses a vanguard propulsion system, something based on air displacement and magnets."

Feeling confident in the abilities of her military administrator, Tess leaned back, removing her reading glasses. "Needless to say, I want to go ahead with a national press release acknowledging the *Truman* incident and its reported causes."

Melvin Knoll nodded as the President continued:

"Let the cat out of the bag, Melvin. And then I'll set up a State Of The Union Address. Let's throw our cards onto the table."

Melvin continued nodding agreeably. "I think that's wise, Tess."

After discussing the general points of the press release, Contessa suggested a forthcoming summit to be scheduled between the Big Eight, as well as China and Russia. Her stance of world solidarity was prudent, and as the President dictated a few personal notes, the satellite phone in her armrest console blurped to life.

Tess took the emergency call, and remained silent as the voice droned in her ear.

"Thank you," said the President after a moment. "Keep me posted on all developments."

She hung up and turned to Secretary Knoll.

"It started about an hour ago, when two of our Los Angeles Class submarines began tracking a battery of unusual readings along the southeast coast of the States. It now appears that the *Truman* wasn't successful after all."

"What are you talking about, President Brice?" asked the Secretary of Defense, a tense look on his face.

"We have just come under attack, Secretary Knoll. We are officially at war."

# 51
# Tokyo Bay, Japan

Cloud cover over the bay was minimal and Mount Fuji stood majestically in the distance, a snow capped volcano of Ice-Age beginnings. At Haneda International Airport all outbound flights had been abruptly cancelled, and the Japanese Capital continued to receive aircraft ordered to return, as well as those unable to find an open airfield at points throughout the south Pacific.

On the island of Honshu, the National Diet Building was in full session and members of the Japanese assembly were discussing the mounting crisis. The legislative epicenter showed no signs of its dark history, of the scars it received in 1923 when a massive earthquake crumbled the capital, or when Allied bombers ravaged the nation   twenty-two years later.

It was a new and contemporary Japan.

Out in Tokyo Bay the fishing trawler *Hideki* was chugging slowly out to sea, its diesel engines blubbering rhythmically across the blue expanse. Anasi Gensho was sitting on the bridge of the fifty-foot trawler. He would later testify before the Diet as to what he witnessed.

"It rose out of the water like a dragon!"

The giant alien apparition then began moving silently across the waves, its light sensors scanning the skies above, as well as the seas below.

At first, Anasi thought he was seeing an American nuclear submarine breaking the surface, and remembered the Japanese tourists killed in Hawaiian waters at the end of the 20th Century, when an American *Trident* broke the surface unexpectedly.

But rather than bobbing to the surface like a large cork, the vessel continued to rise, and was suddenly hovering above Anasi's boat.

Then, after a bright flash of lights, it began moving toward the capital city of Tokyo.

Belts of energy shot from its hull and whirled towards the Imperial Palace before descending rapidly onto the *Ginza,* Japan's immense shopping district. The colored hoops swept down with great force, blowing across buildings in a hot radioactive wind.

At the *Edobashi* interchange more colored hoops appeared, smashing the highway and setting ribbons of traffic ablaze. And at Waseda University colored rings touched the campus with hurricane force, sweeping away a large portion of the school's roof and sending its eastern wall crumbling to the ground.

But the most damaged was incurred along the shopping district known as the *Ginza.* A colored hoop appeared over the cluttered causeways and the conical *San-ai* building was vaporized, its lighted marquee reading Mitsubishi Electric, blown to dust.

And the alien craft was not acting alone.

In the southeast Pacific Ocean a second foreign vessel appeared off the Hawaiian Islands. It rose from the sea off the coast of Molokai, sweeping towards Maui like an enormous wagon wheel. Colored hoops swept across the *Iao* Valley, the vast crater being the world's largest dormant volcano. The hoops radiated over the *Haleakala* National Park and crashed onto *Lahaina,* the very first capital of the Hawaiian kingdom.

Boats were smashed at their moorings, and startled surfers and beach combers gazed skyward as the rainbows swept down.

Sugar fields and pineapple groves were immediately vaporized.

A third vessel broke the surface of the Atlantic off the coast of Havana, Cuba, and a fourth struck the South Beach section of Miami.

The attack had begun.

# 52

The White House aide had remained at his post. And as the crisis unfolded, Douglas Rollins wandered through the empty halls of the Pennsylvania Avenue dwelling like a sleepwalker, occasionally listening to Fox News dole out details of the *Truman* incident. He knew the White House was an attractive target to terrorists, but he also knew that this new enemy could circumvent the Secret Service and irradiate the capital with little problem.

*And if I die here, at least I get the full enchilada,* thought Douglas wryly, referring to expiration benefits and burial assistance available through the federal government.

But his wry humor quickly passed, and Douglas froze when he heard the voice issuing from the television in the next room. He'd heard the distinct chime of a Fox News Alert, and Bill O'Reilly's voice suddenly echoed down the hall.

"Ladies and Gentlemen, it now appears that the United States is under attack! Miami and Hawaii are just a few of the targets which have been struck, and as this crisis develops we'll be sending you pictures!"

Douglas sank into a chair and gazed at the barrel vaulted ceiling in the Truman Study. He didn't need to see the footage. It had turned ugly. The situation suddenly reminded the White House aide of *Torah! Torah!* And although there wasn't an enormous meteor to worry about, the situation suddenly seemed to carry the same life or death implications, the same dark and foreboding portent.

But this was no game.

Douglas suddenly felt compelled to draw up the video puzzle on his computer screen, but knew how insane it would appear to the occasional *Secret Service* agent sweeping along the White House corridors. He instead envisioned the game's narrator reciting the dreadful circumstances.

He could see the meteor clearly now, a rock the size of Alaska, spinning toward the Earth with reckless fatalism.

And then he suddenly saw the solution, as well.

*Three space shuttles, each carrying a compliment of three six-megaton warheads.*

*The string of deployment.*

*The Line of Angels.*

His mind seemed to align the defense with ease. He wouldn't destroy the meteor, rather, alter its course, and the ensuing shock waves from the string of devices would push it entirely off its course heading.

Douglas was surprised when he suddenly remembered a billiard game once played back in college.

He was eyeballing the Eight Ball and made the perfect hit. The Eight rolled lazily toward the pocket, just the right amount of speed and pitch. But Roger Munson, a classmate as well as a sore loser, dropped down, his chin only inches from the green felt, and began blowing as hard as he could. The Eight suddenly slowed and arced away from the pocket, enough to miss the mark cleanly.

There had been a lesson in there somewhere.

Again, Douglas began to hear the voice of Bill O'Reilly droning from the next room:

"...Monterrey, Venezuela, Tokyo, Maui, and Miami have now all reported sightings and attack! Ladies and Gentlemen, we don't want to cause any undue alarm, but this is looking very serious...!"

Again, his mind raced with information, mathematical equations, solvent solutions...

*...Tokyo, Miami, Maui, Caracas, Monterrey.*

*Line of Angels.*

*Monterrey, Caracas, Maui, Miami, Tokyo.*

Like a map, his mind began to visualize the scattered cities now under attack. And then he saw something else.

*Tropic of Cancer.*

Douglas reached for a secured telephone line.

"Get me the President."

# 53
# Somewhere In Omaha

Contessa Brice would address the Nation from the confines of the Strategic Air Command bunker. And although the SAC location was a guarded secret, Tess maintained direct contact with a wide range of governing officials, including the entire compliment of her cabinet and the leaders of the House and Senate respectively.

But it was Defense Secretary Melvin Knoll that occupied most of her ear.

"So far we're just shooting holes in the sky," began Secretary Knoll. "Tomcats and Hornets can't get near them. And we have no idea where they'll strike next."

The President remained silent.

"Phoenix appears to be effective at close range," continued Knoll, flipping through a Pentagon report. "But it's nearly impossible to get close enough, fast enough."

President Brice understood the disadvantage, but she didn't quite know how to respond.

"There are at least five of them," added Adam Kensington. The NSA chief was seated across from Knoll. "And they're avoiding our carriers like the plague. At least we know they bleed just like we do."

"And I think they may be marginally surprised by our resilience," rejoined Secretary Knoll. "And maybe a little frightened, as well. It's possible that they've never encountered a race as resilient as us. They may have roamed through the eons united and uncontested, without many significant military victories to their credit."

"Like fat and happy pirates!" chimed Kensington.

"Have there been any new attacks on the country?" asked Tess, turning abruptly to Secretary Knoll.

"No new attacks," replied Melvin. "But clusters of sightings are still being reported from the aforementioned areas. They seem to be hanging around to admire their handiwork."

"I want brown-outs scheduled for all coastal cities," began the President decidedly. "Let's not give them too much to shoot at."

Knoll nodded, and passed the order to a subordinate who immediately conveyed the order to Washington.

Then the phone call came from Washington. The President took it herself and listened in silence.

After a moment she said: "Thank you, Douglas. Let me know if you come up with any more keen observations."

Everyone was studying the President intently.

"Douglas Rollins has identified an interesting cooincidence," began Contessa, gazing down at the map table. "They seem to be striking targets exclusively along the Tropic of Cancer."

"A one-thousand-mile radius," began Secretary Knoll, leaning over the lighted map table. "Perhaps they need to stay along the belt for communication reasons."

"Or maybe to facilitate their propulsion systems," surmised a Marine colonel. "Or maybe they're using our sun for fuel?"

"Get the entire Atlantic Fleet to patrol the line," replied the President, remembering the horrific loss of the *Truman*. "But we need to find another way to attack along the international perimeter. Our carriers can't do it alone."

"The new Mark 50?" spluttered Kensington.

For a moment, no one spoke.

"Hades was built for high speed interception," added the NSA chief with a ring of optimism.

"I don't think so," spluttered the Marine colonel. "They're being housed thousands of miles from the Tropic of Cancer. The Mark 50 might work, but that's only if those vessels happen across the Bering Strait!"

"They could be an ideal weapon if we could find another means of deployment."

The windowless room again fell silent.

"What about the Blackbird?" asked Tess, turning suddenly to Secretary Knoll.

The SR-71 was an unusual, yet pertinent suggestion. Mothballed almost as soon as it was christened, the SR-71 was still one of the fasted aircraft on the planet, with high altitude, long-range capabilities.

"We could dispatch Blackbirds on reconnaissance flights around the globe, using the Tropic of Cancer as its flight path. Their ram-jets could run them up to an adequate launching altitude. We could just sit and wait."

"And the Scorpions could do the rest," chimed in Secretary Knoll. "I'm willing to bet I can get half a dozen Blackbirds up within the next forty-eight hours."

Tess's eyes traced along the Tropic of Cancer, the imaginary line running along the waist of the planet. "The *SR-71* might be the only thing remotely capable of getting off a clean shot. It seems like a good gamble."

*Five enemy aircraft, against six Blackbirds,* thought Tess nervously. *My White House Chief of Staff might call this a Solvent Solution.*

"AWACS can provide aerial assistance," advised Adam Kensington. "They're already in the air."

Tess was suddenly feeling a bit more empowered, and not so utterly defenseless. At least not as powerless as previous administrations had been in light of these advanced predators. America was making quick strides into the *Modern Age.*

It was a start.

Contessa Brice turned to her Secretary of Defense.

"Put it together, Melvin."

Melvin Knoll was on a secured line seconds later.

# 54

President Contessa Brice attended church regularly.

But under the circumstances, Tess wanted to bring the church to her.

Reverend Philip Barker, of the Omaha Methodist Church, was seated in the bunker's reception area. And minutes after arriving he was led to an inner sanctum to perform the sacrament of Holy Communion. After receiving the Holy Ghost, a ceremony in which her entire entourage participated, the President spent a few moments alone with the reverend.

"Perhaps they don't have gods of their own," began Tess in a whisper. "My men seem to think they resemble a colony of ants, or hornets. I don't feel we have any place among them."

"If I am not mistaken," began the reverend solemnly. "Hostile action has already been perpetrated?"

"Yes, Reverend," began Tess. "But we drew first blood. And until we can find a way to communicate with them, we are staring down the barrel of a gun. I would love to call a truce and roll out the red carpet. But if we lower our guard, especially now, we become dangerously vulnerable."

Reverend Barker opened the Bible at the New Testament and turned to Matthew 7:16. He cleared his throat.

"'Ye shall know them by their fruits. Do men gather grapes of thorns, or figs of thistle?'" he recited, before closing the book and folding his hands.

No. They didn't.

*What the visitors had gathered were mounds of corpses.*

"What about the American people," she continued intently. "I don't want to create a panic, but they have a right to know what's going on."

"I think we already know, President Brice," replied the reverend, smiling. "Like a responsible parent we must communicate dangers tactfully."

She listened pensively, a retrospective gaze in her eyes.

Reverend Barker then handed her his personal Bible.

"Tell them the truth," crackled the wizened voice. "You won't be able to conceal it from them forever. Perhaps it is time for the People to purify their own convictions and establish some form of solidarity. I think President Reagan said it best."

Tess looked up expectantly. "Do you think he knew?"

The reverend shrugged. "He may have had some pretty strong evidence. I guess until now we tried to ignore such a calamitous possibility, and so we buried our heads."

The reverend then paused, before adding: "For the People, it will be a dead reckoning of sorts."

Tess nodded. "I guess it is time to do that."

She finally felt a pang of clarity. It wasn't hard to know them by their fruits. She remembered the toxic cocktails, and couldn't get their horrific heads out of her mind.

And she distinctly remembered the Komodo Dragon analogy.

Indeed, Contessa would know them by their fruits.

And she would wheel out the entire American Battlewagon.

# 55

As Contessa Brice prepared for her State of the Union Address, Mark and Tatiana were on the other side of the country, checking into a New Jersey hotel room.

New York City was officially closed, for all intents and purposes, and Mayor Bloomfield had raised the city's Terror Alert Status to Severe. Bridges were closed, as well as the Lincoln Tunnel, and subway service came to a screeching halt.

But Mark and Tatiana could still see the Manhattan skyline from across the Delaware River, though much of its customary effulgence now absent.

It was a good thing they'd left India when they did. Mark and Tatiana had boarded the very last flight from London to New York. And when they were two-thirds of the way across the Atlantic, the FAA suspended all commercial flights departing the country, and along each coast airports thronged with frightened travelers and returning aircraft.

And the sightings, almost exclusively along the Tropic of Cancer, were occurring almost every hour.

Shortly after arriving at the Newark Day's Inn, following the seven hour drive from Bangor, Maine where they'd eventually landed, Tatiana arranged a meeting with the Smithsonian Institute and, after contacting a Berlin associate, even established a verbal agreement with *National Geographic.* Everything was scheduled to be finalized within the next few days; and just before the telephones went dead, Mark took things a step further, deciding to blow the lid off the story.

And he had no idea of just how big the story would splash.

After convincing Tatiana to go public with her research, Mark contacted WJT-TV, a local New Jersey newscast. After a convincing explanation as to the situation, a reporter from the syndication agreed to meet with them to conduct a field interview.

And only moments after arriving, the WJT investigator was on the telephone to New York. Just moments after that, executives from NBC's *Today Show* were calling the room.

"My producer, the Big Boss, would love to air your story," began the network representative. "Even as early as tomorrow. We will send a car in the morning. Can you be ready at five am?"

Mark assured him that they would.

Neither Mark nor Tatiana would be able to sleep that night, and they both knew it. And instead of going into the bedroom for some much needed rest, Mark hurried to a corner liquor store and purchased a bottle of wine and a pint of Jack Daniel's bourbon. He returned promptly to the hotel room and stepped onto the balcony. Although the brown-out remained in effect, New York's skyline remained something to behold.

Tatiana approached Mark holding a candle.

"At least it's quiet," she said in a whisper. "When you first mentioned the words New York, I thought we would be walking into bedlam and pandemonium."

Mark smiled, but thought: *The calm before the storm.*

Although she'd had several glasses of wine, Tatiana looked very unsettled, and Mark tried to put her mind at rest.

"You have no need to worry, Tatiana. You are safe now. Just stay calm, at least through tomorrow, and let me handle the business part of it."

He then handed her another glass of Chablis.

"Congratulations, Ms. Borosky. Welcome to Your Fifteen Minutes."

Tatiana took the glass. "But I am not even finished my research!"

"Oh, yes you are," intoned Mark evenly. "At least for now. Let the authorities handle it, Tatiana. This has become much more than anyone could have expected."

Now the weary anthropologist was nodding, and her eyes drifted back to the Manhattan skyline. "You are right, Mark. And thank you for helping me *vis* everything. None of *zis* would have been possible *vis*out you."

Mark smiled and reached for her hand. "Just tell the People what you know. And relax."

They left the balcony and went to the bedroom. Tatiana was still carrying the candle, her Hittite dissertation becoming an abstract memory.

They were caught up in a drama beyond the scope of their own comprehension.

And a part of them didn't want to comprehend.

# 56
# Rockefeller Plaza
# New York City

The studio makeup "specialist" was lightly powdering her nose, and Tatiana could see the balding producer instructing a cameraman from across the cavernous room.

"Just relax," began the makeup lady. "Pretend you're talking to your best friend. Don't worry, Katie will make you feel right at home."

Tatiana swallowed heavily. Right before leaving the hotel the Smithsonian had called and made her an enormous offer. If she could find it in her heart to 'donate' her research to the museum in Washington D.C., she'd never have to work again. And even as they were entering Rockefeller Plaza, passing the Atlas sculpture at the main entrance, she could see the crowd swelling curiously around the building.

NBC was expecting record-breaking ratings.

Tatiana tried to remain calm as the balding producer suddenly began speaking to her. But she couldn't seem to connect any meaning to his words. Her eyes began drifting to a lighted news desk, and she could see Katie Couric talking with an audio man. She then saw Matt Lauer approaching, a script clutched in his hand. All three *Today Show* employees turned and looked at Tatiana; Matt began waving, a crooked grin on his face.

Things were moving incredibly fast now, and Tatiana's mind was swimming like a school of frantic minnows.

She was suddenly sitting across from Katie, the director's chair providing an uncomfortable perch.

The set director cried out: *"And 5, 4, 3, 2,...We're Live!"*

Katie smiled into a camera. "We're back, Ladies and Gentlemen, and with us now is Tatiana Borosky, an anthropologist who was actually on the scene in India when all of this began."

Katie then turned to the Ukrainian scholar.

"Okay, Tatiana, tell our viewers at home what you've brought with you and where you found these incredible artifacts."

Tatiana began squirming in her seat.

"I went to India from Ukraine to study the Hittite migration into the Indus Valley," began the anthropologist reservedly, feeling the heat of the overhead stage lights. "My dissertation was entitled, 'Lost People In A Lost World.' Many times…"

"That sounds very interesting," interrupted Katie, crossing a plump leg. "But why don't we go ahead and show the viewers what you've discovered. My producer has assured me that what you have is quite literally out-of-this-world."

Tatiana looked to Mark, who was standing just off the set. "Very well," she began, motioning to her lover. "I have not yet given him a name, but we can call him *Everest*, after the mountain."

Mark began wheeling the dolly across the stage, through the network of wires cluttering the floor. Again, Tatiana the Magician was at work, and Mark felt like her trusty assistant.

Then, without further delay, Mark yanked off the sheet which had draped the skeletal assembly.

Gasps were heard throughout the studio.

Katie looked on with a leering grimace, a hand going across her mouth.

Al Roker was at the other end of the set, staring back from a weather map. *"Holy cow! Look at the meat hooks on that thing!"*

Matt Lauer stumbled as a knee buckled, and Steven Cujacaro's jaw dropped like a free falling elevator.

*"Cut to commercial!"* someone barked.

# 57

They were commissioned during the Johnson Administration, and were mothballed after only a short stint of service. The SR-71 Blackbirds had gone the way of the dinosaur in light of satellite deployment.

But the sleek jets maintained the distinction of being one of the fastest aircraft ever to fly.

And they remained stashed away in the American Intelligence arsenal.

Long, black and constructed of Radar Absorbing Material (RAM) the Blackbird looked like Neptune's spearhead, with a pointed arrowhead configuration and powerful ram-jet engines. Designed to operate in the upper reaches of the atmosphere Blackbird pilots were pseudo-astronauts, feeling the affects of severe gravitational reduction; here, oxygen levels were dreadfully low, necessitating the Blackbird's ram-jet capability, as well as oxygen helmets and *NASA* space suits for decompression. At that altitude the Earth's curvature was noticeable, something that would have made the Medieval World turn on its ear.

And if there was ever a craft which looked as though it belonged in Darth Vader's military arsenal, it was the SR-71.

The first two Blackbirds were launched from Cape Canaveral, Florida and each carried a compliment of twin Mark 50 Scorpion Interceptors attached to wing mounts.

Two more of the sophisticated aircraft were launched from locations in the South Pacific, the first leaving Tokyo at 0400 hours, and a second at 0410, departing Hawaii International Airport, just one mile south of Pearl Harbor.

Their duty was cogent and clear:

High altitude interception.

Seek and destroy.

With as much speed as humanly possible.

Worldwide flight restrictions were rigidly enforced by FAA director

Bobby Ross and, for the most part, the Free World was cooperating.

And it didn't take long for the first results to start reaching the President.

Shortly after a mid-air refueling, an AWACS radar plane over Havana transmitted a weak signal emanating once again from the warm waters off Miami. Ten minutes before their sighting an LA Class attack submarine had begun tracking an underwater signal of identical origin. Navy Chief of Staff William Farlow had already ordered the *USS Ronald Reagan* dispatched to the area, the carrier's air wing having been boosted to over one-hundred F-18 Hornets and F-14 Tomcats.

But it was Blackbird Alamo 1 tracking the signal now.

The SR-71 pilot had been gazing into the inner fringe of space, the inky blue horizon gradually turning to black.

"I think they came for the hot action on South Beach!" cackled the Alamo 1 pilot to a nearby AWACS.

He then flipped a weapon's switch, activating an arming mechanism.

Solid rocket boosters ignited and two Mark 50 Scorpions rifled away into the ionosphere.

The missiles quickly arced to the southeast, and began streaking toward the Tropic of Cancer.

# 58

At night people by the millions became star gazers. Everyone wanted a glimpse of the alien ships which had attacked Miami, Hawaii, and Tokyo, and amateur astronomers and their telescopes were setting up their equipment outside tents and campers, turning the National Emergency into a public spectacle.

From Omaha, the President was star gazing as well, wondering if her ad hoc defense plan would prove even marginally effective. The deployment of nuclear weapons was discussed by the President and her administration, and they were recommended by Secretary Knoll, especially if the Blackbirds failed to prevent subsequent attacks.

But as the federal network bristled with heightened anticipation, something altogether different began approaching the Earth.

And when the situation was clarified, nuclear weapons suddenly became the only prudent solution.

# 59

*Hubble* saw it first.

*That which is coming at you is hardest to see.*

But that which is coming at you at light speed is impossible to see with the human eye; and as the optic imaging system of the *Hubble* Space Telescope gathered the many bits of information, the color computer graphics began rolling off the printer in long sheets, graphic lines depicting synchronized energy and movement through both time and space.

And as the fragments of light were gathered, categorized and represented onto the computer screen, Dexter Moss knew he was studying the incredible.

"We're actually looking into the past," began Moss excitedly.

The Alpha Centauri star system was in his sights now, and the molecular disturbances indicated approaching traffic originating from that parsec.

The NASA astronomer began feverishly jotting a series of notes.

"They are four light years away, but their course heading, direction and speed is something well beyond our scope of understanding!"

*Hubble's* sophisticated lens got it all.

And the deep space phenomenon would arrive faster than anyone could have imagined.

And it was not alone.


Nearly five light years away, inside the Alpha Centauri planetary belt, three suns were locked in a perpetual waltz. A middle-aged yellow giant was tightly flanked by two younger white stars, and this phenomenon of solar triplets quadrupled the energy created by Earth's single yellow star.

Near the moon known as Johar, a second large black vessel turned slowly toward the flicker of light in the distance. Earth's Sun was only a pinprick in the black expanse of space. Earth's distant solar system was a midget compared to the 57 planets orbiting Alpha Centauri, and with over four-hundred colonized moons, the alien race had been efficient with their given circumstances.

And as another large spacecraft settled into its transportation launch position, a third appeared from behind the moon Johar. Resembling a giant horseshoe crab, with its spiked tail, the craft prepared for its chance to *nutrate*. It turned slowly in silence, its long pointed tail beginning to elongate.

Then the vessel vanished in a ball of light.

The third ship then moved into the *Krygonese* launching position.

And then a fourth.

# 60

President Brice was staring blankly at Melvin Knoll, watching the purse of his thin lips as he continued his bizarre monologue. Contessa couldn't believe what she was hearing, and she was expecting to wake up at any second. Then she could begin her day, addressing budget cuts as well as her Educational Program with House Speaker Philbin, who would immediately begin rambling about Social Services and Welfare roles. Douglas, her dear friend and faithful White House Chief of Staff, would greet her with her day's itinerary, and Jonah Weintraub would assure her that the entire perimeter was secure.

But Douglas and Jonah were back in Washington.

And Contessa's itinerary was painfully present.

"A total of four are coming this way," began Melvin Knoll. "But, all considered, I think we're lucky to at least have the chance to see them coming. It's an unprecedented advantage."

Then, like a tour guide through a mortuary, Adam Kensington began to elucidate the nightmare:

"They're four light years away and closing, using some unexplained mode of space travel. It's also possible that they're riding a wormhole or seam through the universe, like a surfer would ride a wave. Our boys at NASA say we'd better start to batten down the hatches."

*Hatches?*

"Just what do you think a *Defcon-1 is* supposed to be?" replied Tess, suddenly coming out of her gloomy reverie.

"Is there any way to prevent their entry into our atmosphere?" she continued hotly, turning to Knoll.

"I imagine that would depend on their means and method of entry," commented the Secretary of Defense. "And only after they begin the process of deceleration will we have a better picture. They're certainly not going to touch down at that current rate of speed. That travel mode is to just move them around."

As the President considered her limited options, the U.S. Coast Guard was recovering enormous pieces of an alien craft off the Coast of Miami, something the Alamo 1 had shot down somewhere between Cuba and the Bahamas.

"And there's still nothing we can do until they get here," remarked Kensington. "We should focus our energies on the ones already present."

"There are approximately four remaining out there," added Kensington.

"Plus the four on the way in," commented Knoll.

*Four of what?* wondered Tess, approaching the map table. *And will they have the same affinity for the Tropic of Cancer?*

"I think we should fully stack the line," began Secretary Knoll. "Throw everything onto the belt. A goal line defense. The best we can do at this stage is maximize our presence."

"We'll need full International cooperation from the pertinent nations," began Kensington.

"Then get Secretary Crofton on the phone," ordered Tess, turning then to her NSA director. "Adam, find out how many shuttles we can deploy in orbit over the next few days. I want this sent to NASA top priority. Our mere presence in space could prove extremely useful at this time."

Then, like a stalking feline, she turned back to Secretary Knoll. "Keep sending up the Blackbirds, Melvin. And then get me my White House Chief of Staff. I think I'd like to ask him a few questions."

She then forced a smile. "Whose got a damn cigarette?"

# 61

It came in as a sub-atomic blur, a transfiguration of antimatter, an equally and corresponding set of opposite particles, an inversion of matter. As the enormous ship began collecting itself, slowing significantly, a trail of radioactive rings emanating from deep space behind it.

The giant alien ship was straight out of a *Battlestar Galactica* pilot, and moved past Pluto with sensors sweeping the planet's gassy surface. Still moving at one tenth the speed of light, it passed Jupiter and continued its surveillance, on-board mapping systems now guiding the vessel electronically.

The orb of Earth sparkled off in the distance, a rotating blue marble.

NASA officials were gazing right back; and for the first time two electric eyes, from two completely removed races, were staring intently at one another.

The Houston control room suddenly erupted in a roll of disjointed jeers.

"They're here!" someone called out.

But rather than crashing into the Earth's atmosphere, the alien craft did something totally unexpected.

As heavy cranes fastened the space shuttle *Baltimore* onto the launch pad at Cape Canaveral, the enormous ship swept toward the Earth's moon, cruising up from the dark side and sweeping the cratered surface with a prism of sensors. It then dropped toward the gray surface, slowing now to Mach 2, and descending.

Suddenly moving at a slow creep, in landed gently onto the moon's surface, a giant puff of solar dust billowing around it.

# 62

"The first one just landed on the moon," began Secretary Knoll. "I assume it's waiting for the others to catch up."

Nothing surprised her anymore.

President Brice was sitting at her desk, the bunker's whirring ventilation fans having a hypnotic affect on her. It was all the working of Fate. Just as Rome had fallen, just as Napoleon had fallen at Waterloo, just as Hannibal had fallen, and Alexander, so too might America.

But just as sure as the sun would rise, so too would America's Great Shield.

"Don't leave any bullets in the gun, Melvin" began Tess, turning to Secretary Knoll. "Even if this doesn't initially go our way, I want to use every tool in the toolbox."

Melvin Knoll nodded. "On that, you can count, President Brice."

"The second craft should be here in about two days," began Kensington assuredly. "It's beginning to look like they'll assemble before doing whatever it is they came here to do."

"Just like D-Day," agreed Secretary Knoll. "Only this time we're the ones holding the beaches."

"At their current speed, all four should be in position in five days, 2 hours, fifteen minutes," added Kensington. "And it's likely they'll resemble the first craft."

"What's the shuttle situation?"

"We've got three on location at Canaveral now," began Melvin Knoll. "*Baltimore* is already on the pad. She'll be the first to go up."

"Let's put the brakes on for a moment," began the President, turning slowly to Secretary Knoll. "If these ships indeed decide to assemble in the same vicinity, we may be able to get them all at once."

There was a pause.

"It's one hell of a possibility," agreed the secretary after a moment.

"And I may have someone uniquely qualified to answer a few of our questions," continued President Brice.

"Get me the White House. I want to talk to Douglas Rollins."

And during the next five days, two hours, and fifteen minutes, as predicted by *NASA* scientists, the remaining three alien craft entered Earth's solar system before assembling on the moon.

Secretary Knoll alerted his boss.

"Their strike force is complete, President Brice. It's D-Day."

Tess forced a smile. "Throw everything, Melvin."

# Book III

# A Queen's Gambit

# 63
# Cape Canaveral, Florida

The warheads had arrived by convoy from the Bethesda Naval Air Station; and as soon as the green supply trucks pulled onto the tarmac, the Pentagon's weapons experts went right to work. The delivery buses had been removed from an MX missile installation, and the powerful warheads were installed at Quantico, Virginia. In all, nine six-megaton warheads were scheduled for launch, three going to the *Baltimore,* three to *Raleigh,* and three to the *Charleston.*

And as the *Baltimore* prepared for launch, curious onlookers continued to gather all along the cape. Nearly one million ordinary American citizens took up positions along the Florida beaches, telescopes, picnic baskets, Frisbees, barbeque grills, coolers and lawn chairs at the ready. Tailgate parties abounded, and motorcycle clubs began arriving from Daytona Beach.

And at 1800 hours, all eyes were gazing toward the launch pad.

In the distance stood the space shuttle *Baltimore,* long booster rockets bracketing the vessel. Waiting in hangars less than two miles away were the *Raleigh* and *Charleston,* each equally outfitted for the large scale reaction, and each waiting to be consecutively launched.

Inside the nose of the *Baltimore,* her crew of eight were buckled into their seats. Captain Lucille Lopez was alone in the cargo bay, making a final weapons check. She was inspecting the three orange cones grouped onto the MX delivery bus. After issuing a final clearance, the countdown began. And moments later a ball of orange smoke appeared.

With the entire world watching, the first shuttle was lifted softly into the air.

"And we have lift off!" exclaimed a NASA engineer.

Seconds later, the *Baltimore* was streaking toward space, her fat liquid booster breaking away as the   Second-Phase boosters ignited, pushing the shuttle through the last leg of the Earth's atmosphere. Then the secondary boosters broke free, tumbling back toward the Atlantic Ocean like twin candlepins.

"She's running on secondary engines!" proclaimed the engineer.

"We have a successful launch!"

# 64
# *The* USS Baltimore

Once again, they began floating across the dark side of the moon. Only two-hundred miles beneath the *Baltimore* was the crater of *Osiris,* an immense hole born of an immense meteorite collision, the universal force which gave evolving planets form for function.

The shuttle would emerge into sunlight approximately six hours later, and this time they should sweep directly over the assembly of alien spacecraft.

"We should have the fleet assembled in a matter of hours, *Baltimore,*" came the appraisal from Mission Control. "Hold your pattern and ready your vessel."

Colonel Robert 'Skip' Halford reached for his throat microphone and smiled into a cockpit camera.

"10-4, *Houston.* No problems."

# 65

As mission control began its final countdown for the *Raleigh* launch, the unusual signals were again detected, this time off the beaches of Jacksonville. An AWACs patrolling the coast immediately broadcast the signal to fleet below.

But the *USS Ronald Reagan* would never get there in time.

As jets of steam were drifting up from *Raleigh's* liquid fuel tank, and a pre-ignition flame appeared beneath its nozzle, Mission Control continued its scheduled countdown, 29, 28, 27, 26...

But the enormous wagon wheel suddenly appeared over the Cape, and hundreds of thousands of onlookers shifted their eyes to the north. The sight would have had H.G. Wells rolling over in his grave. Rings of radiation suddenly burst from its rotating black hull, before pulsating toward the launch pad.

NASA's main tower was instantly vaporized by the radioactive wind, along with the launch pad and shuttle assembly, each swallowed in a bright ball of phosphorescence. Air traffic controllers were annihilated, and hangars, runways, parking lots and fuel trucks were swallowed next. A collective howl rolled along the beaches as nearly a million onlookers witnessed the horrific sight that had just taken place before them.

Everything at Cape Canaveral was laid waste.

Another shuttle was gone.

# 66

"*Houston,* this is *Baltimore,*" began Colonel Halford; he was floating through the cockpit now, moving toward a weapons panel mounted to the bulkhead. "We've just completed our fifth orbit around the moon, and we should make our first visual sweep across the target area in about 2 hours, 13 minutes, over."

There was no reply, and the Air Force colonel repeated the message.

"We read you *Baltimore,*" came the tardy reply from Houston, Texas. "But we have just lost your escorts. Do you copy? Over."

"Good God!" gasped Major Lopez. "What happened?"

"They hit the Cape just as the *Raleigh* was preparing for lift-off. The entire coast of Florida is out. You will be doing this alone, *Baltimore.*"

The colonel glanced at his second in command.

"Did you hear that? We're it, Major."

The co-pilot genuflected.

"Then let's do what we came to do," she added intently.

# 67

"President Brice, three of our Atlantic satellites have just been lost," began the *NASA* engineer.

Contessa Brice was talking live to a video feed from Houston; the large color monitor was situated in the center of her office. "It appears that they are attempting to neutralize our eyes."

"To blind us," commented Secretary Knoll solemnly.

"Here it comes," began Tess, standing. "What is the status of the *Baltimore?*"

"They're coming up on their final sweep now."

Contessa Brice turned to Melvin Knoll.

"May God be with them."

# 68

The space shuttle *Baltimore* broke slowly into the crest of sunlight and the pock-marked face of the moon appeared, it's many craters and divots reminding Colonel Halford of a story he'd once told his youngest son. Skip had professed to Karl that the moon's divots were proof that God played golf.

A lot.

There was an eerie silence over his headset.

"Where are they?" asked Captain Henderson, drifting weightlessly to another starboard window in the shuttle's cargo bay.

"I don't know," replied the mission commander. "Let's get the bay doors open. Is everything okay back there?"

"10-4, Colonel," replied Major Lopez.

"There they are, Colonel!" prattled the excited   co-pilot.

Just seconds later the entire crew was gazing at the alien spacecraft through the reinforced Plexiglas. The vessels were clustered in the moon's crater *Nomar*, arrayed in a neat and clustered phalanx.

"Why are there only three?" asked Captain Henderson.

"*Houston,* we only have three subject targets," began Colonel Halford into his radio. "One may have gotten away, over."

There was a pause.

Colonel Halford began to repeat the message. "Houston…"

"We copy, *Baltimore,*" came the heated reply.

It was the voice of the President of the United States. "You are to execute your delivery assignment immediately! They are preparing to attack us!"

Colonel Halford suddenly looked as if he'd just swallowed a lethal dose of epinephrine; his eyes went wide and his hand began to quaver. He was staring blankly out the window, his face turning pale.

After a moment of complete silence, he glanced around at his crew:

"We only have one shot, People! Let's do it right!"

In silence, the cargo bays to the *Baltimore* were opened and the delivery bus was released from the bay, tumbling end over end toward the moon.

Skip Halford watched the module as it sped away, and his eyes darted to the weapons console. His fingers fell on a panel of switches, and he began to fondle a splay of buttons and toggles.

And then a blade of reality cut through him. The entire planet was depending on a single bull's eye shot. Had the warheads been wired correctly? Had they *reattached* all of the electronics correctly? Would there be enough time?

Everything had been executed with such haste.

Of all the places and all the crisis over the Ages, this was no time for human error to rear its head.

A voice suddenly crackled in his headset. It was Major Lopez.

"Weapons check?"

"Arming now!" replied Colonel Halford, as three lights began blinking on his instrument panel. He pressed each of the buttons, arming each of the warheads.

The delivery bus was now a tiny dot in the expanse of space.

And loaded for much more than bear.

"*Houston,* ten minutes for detonation," began Halford into his radio headset.

"Well done, *Baltimore,*" came the reply from Earth. "Now get the hell away from there!"

# 69

Colonel Halford was gazing intently at the targets situated on the solar horizon. The silver wash of sunlight cast eerie shadows across the moon's craggy surface, and the alien vessels could be seen grouped neatly inside the familiar *Nomar* crater.

Then, at 0814 hours, Skip lost sight of the vessels in a great flash of light. Then a second, and a third. Three mushroom clouds fought furiously for room to expand, and the targets were swallowed instantly in the rolling man-made vortex. The face of the moon was suddenly obscured with solar dust and tumbling rocks. Visibility became zero and the crew of the *Baltimore* began to hear tiny pieces of debris striking the heat shields of the shuttle. Everyone remained silent as radioactive shock waves buffeted the *Baltimore*.

"Did you see that?" barked Colonel Halford into the throat microphone.

"Roger, Colonel," replied the co-pilot. "I think we scored a touchdown!"

"But the game's not over," commented the mission commander. "Remember, one of them got away. I hope we weren't too late!"

"Sounds a little like *Midway,*" commented Major Lopez, before beginning a damage assessment on the *Baltimore*.

Halford smiled as he communicated the results to NASA, the President, and the citizens of the planet Earth.

"*Houston,* this is *Baltimore. Jericho* appears to be a success. All three warheads have been deployed and successfully detonated over the target area."

"Congratulations, *Baltimore!*" came the robust reply into his headset. "A job well done!"

Halford's eyes were sweeping through space. "But we think a fourth one is headed your way, over."

"Affirmative, *Baltimore,*" came the immediate reply. "We're tracking it now."

# 70

It burned through the Earth's atmosphere at Mach 15, a searing ball of glowing energy; the Blackbirds never had a chance to engage. Nor did the Tomcats. The alien ship was fast, flaring through the ionosphere like a blast furnace, its hull glowing red from the intense friction of re-entry.

The alien warship appeared over the Del/Mar/Va peninsula without incident and began slowing, a streak of light over the Chesapeake Bay. As it began decelerating to Mach 5, several American fighter pilots attempted to maneuver and engage; but the vessel streaked toward the ground in a vertical plunge, appearing in the skies over Washington, D.C. seconds later.

It came through uncontested.

A siren wailed across the Nation's Capitol, and the streets quickly became deserted. The spacecraft streaked boldly down and attempted a landing in the center of Lincoln Park.

The dismount was not a picture of beauty. The enormous craft, clearly unaccustomed to landing on the atmospheric conditions of planet Earth, came in too fast and haphazardly, skidding across Lincoln Park like a ploughshare, digging up tracts of manicured lawn and ripping up gas pipes, sprinkler systems and sewage lines. As the smoke gradually cleared, and television cameras began rolling, Apache helicopters swept in from the south, their gunners strafing the smoking craft with 20mm mini-guns.

Waves of energy, resembling large smoke rings, began pulsating from the ship's black hull, causing each of the helicopters to lose power and crash into and around the Potomac River.

It was now the 1st Armored Division that raced toward it, clattering down Independence Drive like modern charioteers, muzzles flashing repeatedly through the cherry blossoms.

Another wave of energy shot from the vessel's hull, but a pair of *Abrams* tanks raced imperviously through the walls of light, steel treads tearing up the asphalt along Pennsylvannia Avenue. Hummers and Bradley Fighting Vehicles appeared along the opposite end of the park, racing breakneck toward the alien craft, which was now preparing to disgorge something.

The alien ship suddenly glowed brilliantly, cascades of light emanating from its hull. Then a portion of its tapered hull simply vanished, and something ran through the translucent portal and lumbered onto the grass of the park.

It moved like a ten-foot gorilla, awkward yet fast. The hairless animal had long, gangling limbs, with thick muscles twitching all along an immense, sinuous body. The giant beast roared, a call to others, and soon a herd was lumbering through the park like a pack of giant hyenas.

But they were not the soldiers, rather the attack dogs. Seconds later, lances of light burst from the hull and small hovercraft appeared overhead, lasers firing from tiny beacons mounted to glowing hulls.

These were the soldiers.

Army Rangers of the 76th Infantry opened fire, and their automatic weapons proved effective at short range. *TOW* anti-tank missiles soon began shredding the park, and the battle lasted nearly eight hours.

The final shot was fired at 6:04 pm, when an Apache Hellfire missile struck the vessel with its portal open, sending walls of fire spreading throughout the vessel's interior.

A smoky haze whirled over the District. And Lincoln Park was littered with the carcasses of bizarre animals and burning hovercraft.

And yet not one American soldier had died during the assault.

# 71
# Two Months Later

*The White House is a little too quiet,* she thought, walking slowly toward the Lincoln Study.

And Tess often pondered the morality and spiritual implications of her actions. Could there have been a more peaceful solution to the situation, another way, something that she may have overlooked?

*There had to be.*

And then, for some reason, she began to think of the Middle-East. For the first time in her life, Contessa Brice could not fathom a solution.

*Perhaps we will always look for a reason to fight, to hate one another.*

She then began to replay the tactics of these unknown adversaries, the approaching warriors which had threatened so much. They didn't seem very battle prone. And it was possible that they had never encountered such a warring People, were not expecting such an effusive and volatile response.

*What had Adam called them? Lazy space pirates? They simply weren't expecting anything like us.*

*Even with inferior machines and weapons, we'd managed to turn them into moon dust with several well-placed nuclear warheads, before butchering them swiftly on the grass of Lincoln Park.*

*Yes, we came as a complete surprise to them. But were the weapons which had saved us mere bi-products of our ruthless barbarity, a symbol of our destructive nature? Surely these advanced travelers didn't know how to effectively cope with our multi-layered weapons systems. Was this really a military victory, or a mere testament to our hostile and destructive nature as human beings. From Mycenae and Troy, to India and Pakistan, Sparta and Athens, Carthage and Rome. The History of Mankind is smeared with blood.*

*Our heroes have been warriors. From Achilles to Schwarzkopf, Nebuchanezzar to Dwight D. Eisenhower, Hannibal to George Bush.*

*Is it merely the hopeless barbarian in us?*

Or was there something more to it?

As she strolled through the Oval Office, Tess thought of the Lincoln bedroom, a room in the White House which contained a copy of the *Emancipation Proclamation*

She was smitten with a chord of optimism.

And then she felt her faith, and hope, and belief returning.

Perhaps it wasn't our taste for blood, as much as our pursuit of independence and freedom that had wrought this victory.

*We have always endeavored to autocratic status, even reaching as far back as Adam and Eve.*

President Contessa Brice began to realize that every war may have actually been waged in the name of liberation and freedom, in one form or another.

And in that philosophy, she would find comfort and solace.

And only then did she begin to realize that America's quick, measured, and overwhelming response was indeed a Just Reaction, as well as a Solvent Solution.

Douglas had said it best.

# 72

Tatiana Borosky never left New York. And she and Mark Black gradually grew apart. The Ukrainian anthropologist purchased a Manhattan condominium overlooking the East River, before going on to write two *New York Times* bestsellers entitled, *The Hittite Gods* and *They Came To The Mountain.* She remained atop the *New York Times Bestseller List* for six consecutive years.

Mark Black, the former Pendleton & Waxler dozer operator, and marginally wealthy from a multitude of tabloid interviews and talk show appearances, moved to a cottage in Malibu. At some point a literary agent from New York had approached him about a six-figure book deal. Mark said he would need at least a few days to think about it.

But as the agent awaited his return phone call, Mark drove to L.A.X. and boarded a plane to Las Vegas. He arrived in *Sin City* around three a.m. and could see the neon glow as the Boeing 767 descended onto the desert runway.

Mark immediately checked into the Mirage Hotel & Casino, and shortly after four in the morning he strolled into the hotel's main gaming room.

Mark ordered a bourbon and Coke, and strolled purposefully up to the Roulette Wheel. As the black marbled danced merrily across the colored wheel, Mark could feel a dormant excitement and anticipation returning. Like a wisp of smoke it curled through his stomach and raced down his arm.

He placed a stack of chips on *Black 16* and glared at the wheel as it began whisking around.

"God help me," he muttered to himself. "For I am powerless."

# Epilogue
# Ten Years Later

From the fires of war, another branch of science was born. And it touched American culture on every level. A new form of space vehicle came to replace NASA's ageing fleet of shuttles; called Arrows, these revolutionary spacecraft were the only manmade vessels capable of reaching beyond the earth's gravitational pull without the need for liquid or solid rocket fuel. The Arrow's sophisticated propulsion system, based on the displacement of 'peripheral atmospheric pressure' would one day allow Earth's astronauts to travel to the furthest reaches of the galaxy in a milli-fraction of the time.

The galaxy, and beyond.

The foreign animals themselves yielded enormous discoveries in medicine. The *Futi's* venom, the deadly cocktail contained in its bite, was found to contain a powerful antigen, used by the animal to protect itself from infection. And when mixed with a saline extract, the new chemical compound improved immunity levels nearly 100 percent, eventually putting AIDS on the endangered species list.

As the world of medicine branched out, industry reaped the benefits as well. General Electric gradually introduced a hovercraft to the public; powered by another unique form of propulsion, these eco-friendly transportation modules allowed civilians to cross the world's oceans in mere minutes.

Three new alloys were added to the atomic particle chart as well, increasing the number of positively charged elements belonging to the chart. And the technologies surrounding them would be studied into and through infinitum.

The chemical and atomic structure of the first, which became known as *AlphaKorum*, was said to curb cancer reproduction, while stimulating DNA

247

and dendrite reproduction.

And *Syfex 1* and *2*, materials possessing high levels of radium and *Kolflex,* were found to be compatible with corresponding neurotransmitters, rendering it useful in the study and treatment of spinal injuries.

Contessa Brice went on to win a second term, this one by a landslide. And after leaving office in 2016, she retired graciously from politics and moved to Martha's Vineyard, to a life of quietude off the coast of Massachusetts.

Her house, a three story Queen Anne, was situated on a hill overlooking a spread of arbors and vines.

Behind her cottage were flowerbeds and vegetables, a garden eclectic enough to make Martha Stewart cry with joy from the confines of her federal cellblock.

Seated at a settee in her enclosed courtyard, Tess began the first lines of her own book, an autobiographical tell-all.

The whole world would know the story.

As told from the White House, by the First-Female-African-American-Republican President ever.

Contessa Brice had gone one up on Cinderella.

But out in deep space, beyond the sweeping orbit of Pluto, and past the argent glow of Alpha Centauri, were the nebulous alien eyes.

Now shielded from the sophisticated stare of radio telescopes, the hidden creatures continued watching the volatile blue planet known as Earth.

And they studied.

And they waited.

And soon, the very next step in the newest arms race was ventured.

# The End

Printed in the United States
24897LVS00003B/269